The Biography of an Idealist

OTHER TITLES IN THE SERIES

Prague Tales
Jan Neruda

Skylark
Dezső Kosztolányi

Be Faithful Unto Death
Zsigmond Móricz

The Doll
Bolesław Prus

The Adventures of Sindbad
Gyula Krúdy

The Sorrowful Eyes of Hannah Karajich
Ivan Olbracht

The Birch Grove and Other Stories
Jaroslaw Iwaszkiewicz

The Coming Spring
Stefan Żeromski

The Poet and the Idiot and Other Stories
Friedebert Tuglas

The Slave Girl and Other Stories on Women
Ivo Andrić

On the cover: "Willows" by Matija Jama, 1909,
National Gallery of Slovenia, Ljubljana

Martin Kačur

The Biography of an Idealist

Ivan Cankar

Translated and with and Introduction
by John K. Cox

Central European University Press

Budapest • New York

First published in Slovenian as *Martin Kačur* in 1907

Published in 2009 by

Central European University Press
An imprint of the
Central European University Share Company
Nádor utca 11, H-1051 Budapest, Hungary
Tel: +36-1-327-3138 or 327-3000
Fax: +36-1-327-3183
E-mail: ceupress@ceu.hu
Website: www.ceupress.com

400 West 59th Street, New York NY 10019, USA
Tel: +1-212-547-6932
Fax: +1-646-557-2416
E-mail: mgreenwald@sorosny.org

ISBN 978-963-9776-41-8
ISSN 1418-0162

This book was published with the support of Trubar Foundation at the Slovene Writers' Association, Ljubljana, Slovenia.

Library of Congress Cataloging-in-Publication Data

Cankar, Ivan, 1876-1918.
[Martin Kacur. English]
Martin Kacur : the biography of an idealist / Ivan Cankar ; translated and with and introduction by John K. Cox.
p. cm. -- (Central European University Press classics, ISSN 1418-0162)
ISBN 978-9639776418 (pbk. : alk. paper)
1. Cankar, Ivan, 1876-1918--Translations into English. 2. Slovenia--Social life and customs--Fiction. 3. Slovenia--Fiction. I. Cox, John K., 1964- II. Title. III. Series.

PG1918.C3M313 2009
891.8'435--dc22

2009002730

Printed in Hungary by
Akadémiai Nyomda, Martonvásár

Contents

Translator's Preface vii

Introduction: Reading Ivan Cankar—Socialism, Nationalism, Esthetics, and Religion after One Hundred Years xi

Part I

Chapter 1 3
Chapter 2 27
Chapter 3 55

Part II

Chapter 1 77
Chapter 2 99
Chapter 3 121

Part III

Chapter 1 143
Chapter 2 165
Chapter 3 189

Translator's Preface

The name of Slovenia's best-known prose writer and dramatist, Ivan Cankar (1876–1918), entered my world while I was in graduate school—through the trope of the national awakener, via chance encounters with his works in those delightful used bookstores in Bloomington and Chapel Hill and by dint of a brief visit to his home village on an early trip to Slovenia. When I actually started reading beyond the parable of the stubborn and star-crossed Jernej, I quickly detected a lot of grit and gristle between the twin icons of Cankar as patriot and Cankar as mystic. There was the bohemian personal life, the jaw-dropping productivity, intriguing satire that embraced the sarcastic and profane, an obsession with the victims of capitalism and ignorance and hypocrisy that bordered on the obscene (yet somehow seemed transcendent), and Aesopian political pronouncements worthy of inclusion in any *fin-de-siècle* or Yugoslav time capsule.

Because there is *so much*, philosophically and esthetically, *to* Cankar, and so much *of* Cankar that remains untranslated, I am elated to be able to join the ranks of the translators who have endeavored to bring parts of

Cankar's oeuvre into circulation in the anglophone world. It is my fervent hope that the publication of this novel will spark meaty discussions among readers, and that more Cankar will find its way into translation soon.

The textual basis for this translation is the 1966 edition of *Martin Kačur: življenjepis idealista*, published by Mladinska knjiga in Ljubljana, with annotations and an afterword by Ignac Kamenik. A small number of textual errors in the Kamenik text were corrected on the basis of the 1967 edition of the novel, edited by Josip Vidmar and published in the third volume of Cankar's *Izbrano delo*, also by Mladinska knjiga.

This book would not have been possible without the friendship and assistance of many people. My special thanks go out to Nick Miller and Linda Kunos for getting this project rolling; to Božidar Blatnik, Katja Sturm-Schnabl, and Erwin Köstler for inspiring me to explore Slovenia and Slovene over the years; to my dear friends Jeff Pennington and Peter Vodopivec for their unstinting advice and material assistance along the way; and, as ever, to my wife Katy and our children, Lilly and Ethan.

I also need to express my appreciation for the support offered during this project by Betsy Birmingham, Alf Brooks, Kevin Brooks, Henry R. Cooper, Jr., Fran Fisher, Sibelan Forrester, Bogdan Rakić, Kelly Sassi, Verena Theile, and the excellent staff of the Interlibrary Loan office at the main library of North Dakota State University.

I believe this is also the place to express my wonder and gratitude in regard to the best lifetime of language teachers imaginable: Frau Fritsch, Marilyn Jenkins Turbeville, Kim Vivian, Doryl Jenkins, Roger Weinstein, Magda Gera, Sibelan Forrester, Anto Knežević, Anka Dušej-Blatnik, Jana Kobav, and Piotr Drozdowski.

This translation is dedicated to Ethan, for all his warm, madcap energy.

John K. Cox
Professor of History
North Dakota State University

Reading Ivan Cankar

SOCIALISM, NATIONALISM, ESTHETICS, AND RELIGION AFTER ONE HUNDRED YEARS

INTRODUCTION

The Caribbean writer Jamaica Kincaid (b. 1949) asserted in her long essay on the history of Antigua that "all masters of every stripe are rubbish, and all slaves of every stripe are noble and exalted."[1] Josip Vidmar, a major literary historian and once the President of the Slovene Academy of Arts and Sciences, declared that Ivan Cankar, in a radically different setting, held analogous views: "whoever is a victim is pure and exalted" and it is the "'humiliated and outraged' of this world" who are "spiritually close to his heart" and receive his "proud melancholy love."[2] This notion certainly captures the spirit of much of Cankar's work; it is, for instance, the driving force in the newly translated novel at hand, *Martin Kačur*, the story of the disastrous degeneration of an idealistic country schoolteacher.

[1] Jamaica Kincaid, *A Small Place* (New York: Farrar, Straus, Giroux, 1988), p. 81.

[2] Josip Vidmar, "Ivan Cankar (1876–1918)." In Ivan Cankar, *My Life and Other Sketches*, transl. Elza Jereb and Alasdair MacKinnon (Ljubljana: Državna založba Slovenije, 1971), p. 10.

For decades, though, the best-known Cankar work to anglophone audiences has been *The Bailiff Yerney and His Rights*, and this work, too, gives voice to the victims of injustice and hopelessness; when the long-time farm-worker Jernej is suddenly driven from the manor, he seeks justice—not pity, mercy, or forgiveness—and ultimately revenge. His arguments are worthy of Gracchus Babeuf in their assertion of right over might and their claims to the fruit of one's own labor. One can read this as class struggle, or national liberation, or, as has been agilely proposed, the designation of Slovenia as a "proletarian nation" worthy of sympathy among internationalist communist and traditional patriotic audiences alike.

But one need only take the short step from the highly symbolic action of Jernej's campaign to the "slum stories" dating from Cankar's time in industrial Vienna to see a very concrete rendering of victimhood in socio-economic terms. The characteristic and quite chilling story "Mimi" (published in Slovene in 1900 but not yet translated into English) is painfully hard to forget: a young girl in the cold city surrounded by hunger, sexual abuse, alcoholism, predatory bosses, and pollution cannot fathom what "crime" she must have committed to deserve a life this denatured and desperate; she finally takes her life by plunging out of the very building that is her prison and the very window that should have been her access to sunshine and flowers. Then there is more incontrovertible evidence of Cankar's social critique: the many war sketches and parables from the end of his life, where a kind of anthropomorphized religion has taken the place of nature as the symbol of the ideal, but in which the militarization and mass destruction of the Great War provide the indispensable setting. Without a doubt Cankar saw it as his tasks to put forth a profound critique of the existing order and to chart a path to renewal. The reader must decide for herself whether Cankar's "relevance" is primarily based on the cause of nationalism, social justice, or spiritual reconciliation.

Reading Ivan Cankar today can be depressing. Surprisingly enough, though, this is a good thing. Time and distance can liberate the reader—if he or she chooses—from many of the categories, accolades, and prisms previously associated with this talented and prolific Slovene prose writer, poet, and dramatist. But the raw emotions of novels like *Martin Kačur* remind us of the enduring affective power of Cankar's work. Indeed this introductory essay will soon enough turn to consideration of Cankar's significance in both political and literary history; in addition, many people are quite used to examining Cankar's work in relation to his psychology, patriotism, and spirituality. But to pick up *The Ward of Our Lady of Mercy* as an introduction to Cankar's oeuvre, to read it, and then to feel profoundly depressed—this is sure testimony of the author's enduring artistry and abiding emotional power.

In the aforementioned novel, we witness a roomful of children slowly dying of disease and untreated handicaps. They are in a convent hospital, a group of about twelve girls, and the duality of life inside and life outside the ward provides the narrative structure of the short novel. But the overarching theme, and the blow that repeatedly, mercilessly, but quietly, clinically, even stoically delivers the emotional punch of the book is the realization that everybody *demands something* from these hopelessly ill and vulnerable girls; everybody is more powerful than they—yet all the grownups desire things and take them, in effect gorging themselves physically and emotionally on the tenderest of victims, many of them their own flesh and blood, all of them potent symbols of ultimate vulnerability. All the adults bring their selfish demands and preconceptions to bear on the young victims, resulting in neglect and exploitation of breathtaking dimensions. The abuse, including rape, visited on the girls (and their mothers, one should add) by men in the outside world is shocking; its description in the book got Cankar in trouble with the censors of his day. But the inside world is equally characterized by this emotional neglect and physical exploitation: drunken fathers on visits seek food and kill the girls' pets; blue-blooded, tight-fisted philanthropists ask coldly for the girls' blessings through prayer; and the Church (while providing reasonably good physical care) demands the sacrifice of their sensuality. Even the case-hardened girls themselves impatiently summon the death of one of their own, the protagonist Malchie, when her lingering passing, so frightfully and graphically presented by Cankar, delays the start of their springtime excursion into the countryside.

Life outside is cruel indeed; Cankar in his naturalistic mode here shows us plenty of examples of even grownups "on strings," buffeted by poverty and corruption. Whatever the root causes of their behavior, the (biological) fathers are the worst: lascivious, drunken, violent, or absent at best. Nonetheless the life outside holds promise, or seems to: sunshine, flowers, birds, church bells, holidays, fluffy snow, carriage rides, room to run, boys…and maybe even faint hopes of a welcoming pair of arms or eyes in a tenuous family setting. But Cankar demonstrates finally, conclusively, that the difference between the outside and inside worlds is just a mirage. And the reason that this book is such an excellent introduction to Cankar's work is because the reader quickly becomes aware of another illusory distinction: that between the sick little girls in the ward and all the adults in the rest of his work and, by easy extension, the rest of us. We need only remember the most poignant scene in *The Ward of Our Lady of Mercy*, with the tragic powerlessness and pathetic dreams of little Minka, so eager to give love and so hungry to receive it and so unaware of all the structural impossibilities of both. But Cankar, as partial as he was to poignant depictions of mothers and children, wants us to feel as deeply about the crushed dreams and harsh socio-economic realities and loneliness of all of humanity.

BIOGRAPHY

Ivan Cankar was born on May 10, 1876, in the village of Vrhnika, not far from Ljubljana. He lived with his parents, Jožef and Neža (née Pivkova), and seven siblings through elementary school. His father was a tailor and the family life far from prosperous. He then went to high school in Ljubljana, then the capital of the southern Habsburg province of Carniola (German *Krain*, Slovenian *Kranjsko*). He lived in hardship in the city, but he proved himself a talented student and began writing poetry. In 1896 he moved to the metropolis of Vienna to study engineering. He quickly gravitated towards philosophy instead, although he never earned his university degree. He learned French and Italian, read widely, and met with friends for intensive discussions of contemporary currents in European literature. For the next fourteen years he resided mostly in Ottakring, a working-class district in Vienna, with some time spent in other parts of the Empire: in and around Ljubljana and also in Pula and Sarajevo, cities in the neighboring South Slavic regions of Croatia and Bosnia. He lived mostly from the advances and proceeds deriving from his writing; despite his prolific output, it was a precarious existence. By 1907 his activities were taking an increasingly political bent, and he ran unsuccessfully for a seat representing Ljubljana in the Austrian parliament. His profession of socialism and Yugoslavism (solidarity among South Slavs) placed him in progressive, if not radical, circles; indeed he was jailed for several months in the fall of 1914 for pro-Serbian views considered dangerous to the Monarchy at war after the assassination of Archduke Franz Ferdinand. Cankar never married but had significant, long-term romantic relationships with a working-class woman in Vienna, Albina Löffler, and then with her daughter, Steffi, and in Ljubljana with Mici Kessler, a student. Cankar died on December 11, 1918, of pneumonia. He is buried in Ljubljana.

In his lifetime, Cankar published an astounding thirty-three books. This number is even more remarkable because his first major work, the poetry collection *Erotika*, appeared in 1899 and his remaining books all appeared before 1917. There were, of course, unpublished and uncollected writings which were gathered after his death, as well as many compilations and re-issues. His thirty-volume *Complete Works*, edited by Anton Ocvirk, was finally brought out over a number of years and was completed in 1976. A major ongoing translation project by the literary historian Erwin Köstler and the Austrian publishing house Drava is making a significant number of Cankar's works available in German. Although translations of Cankar exist in an amazing number of languages, from Hindi and Finnish to Chinese, they include only a small fraction of his works. Today Cankar remains very popular in Slovenia. A major Slovene cultural center and publishing house are named for Cankar; many streets and topographic features are named for him, and a very large banknote bore his image in the early years of independent Slovenia.

THE LITERARY WORKS

Cankar's opus is huge. He compressed a lifetime of writing into less than twenty years and his double-time march through every genre, from poetry and autobiography to short stories and drama, leaves us amazed. But there are grounds for joy as well, for the interested reader will not soon run out of new Cankar to explore.

One of the first thing one notices is that there is, of course, some thematic overlap and some works that lack fermentation time (i.e., smooth editing), but in Cankar's defense one must just as quickly add that he writes not only in different genres but also different modes or styles; there are naturalism, symbolism, and expressionism at the very least in his writing, and they account for some of the different feeling from work to work. It is also no artistic sin to stake out a particular geographic and psychological territory and re-visit and re-work it consistently over the years. Far from a foible, actually—this is part of the characteristic genius of Faulkner, Hardy, Greene, and Kadare. Indeed, Cankar's territory is unique in the anglophone world and is highly moving *and* highly instructive from a historical point of view. But before exploring more of Cankar's unique contributions to Central European literary and political history, it might be worth mentioning, by way of orientation, a few more of the parallels or connections to other writers that today's readers might notice as they make their way through Cankar's works.

There is in Cankar, without a doubt in this historian's mind, a substantial chunk of shared territory with Émile Zola, the great naturalist who chronicled the battered lives of the ordinary men and women of industrializing France both urban and rural. In addition, Cankar's emphasis on the terrors and disappointments—and especially the perfidies—of childhood puts one very much in mind of Graham Greene; the bloody dénouements and pitiless comparisons in his parables and fables about animals and human society remind one of Meša Selimović and other existentialists; his ruminations on Paris as the capital of the mind, true home to all European artists (or not), yield intriguing comparisons to a host of writers from Nietzsche and A.G. Matoš to Danilo Kiš. I think, though, that the most profitable general comparison might be a rather surprising one: George Orwell.[3] Beyond the leftist political stands (think *Homage to Catalonia*), the bohemian personal inclinations (think *Down and Out in Paris and London*), the impulse to chronicle the misery of the new era (think *The Road to Wigan Pier*), and the occasional famous characters from the animal world, the red-letter mutual province is the commitment to brutal honesty, to relentless inquiry and unstinting directness, to the war against hypocrisy and duplicity. The search for self-knowledge and the attempt to lay bare the operating mechanisms of society are everywhere in Cankar, even in the merely "decadent" and oft-anthologized poem "Viennese Evenings." But the fourteenth chapter of Cankar's memoirs[4] puts it in normative methodological terms: it holds a moving plea for honesty of observation in writers and in ordinary mortals, too—and it points clearly to the moral Sword of Damocles hanging over the head of every member of that former group: that "[w]hen we read his confessions,

[3] Nearly every commentator on Cankar has produced a list of parallels, influences, or comparisons; the literary luminaries range from Dostoyevsky and Ibsen to Molière and the Bible. See Vidmar, in *My Life*, p. 7; Avsenik Nabergoj, pp. 262 and 275; Lavrin, in *The Bailiff Yerney*, viii and xi; and Slodnjak, *Ward*, p. 7.

[4] "My Life," in *My Life and Other Sketches* (Ljubljana: Državna založba Slovenije, 1971), pp. 60–64.

we are seized by the feeling which is the most terrible sentence on a writer: we do not believe him."[5] And lest artificial lines be drawn between the political and the personal, let us not forget to be forthright always about our fellow humans and ourselves: "For the heart," wrote Cankar at the end of one of his most famous sketches, "is a righteous judge and knows nothing of great or small…"[6] Orwell is still called by many "the patron saint of common decency" and this epithet would suit Cankar very well also.

Only a small percentage of Cankar's works have been translated into English. There are many worthwhile projects for translators waiting in the wings; perhaps one might single out the novel *Gospa Judit* (Miss Judith, 1904) as especially deserving,[7] or the strange and autobiographical novel of youth, *Grešnik Lenart* (Lenart the Sinner, 1921), or the tale of social exclusion and banditry entitled *Smrt in pogreb Jakoba Nesreče* (The Death and Burial of Jakob the Unfortunate, 1907). The play *Za narodov blagor* (For the Good of the People, 1901) would make interesting reading in Central European political history. Literary and social historians would all benefit from seeing more of what this translator call's Cankar's "slum stories" from Vienna in English. And, last but not least,

[5] *Ibid.*, p. 64.

[6] "A Cup of Coffee," in *My Life and Other Sketches* (Ljubljana: Državna založba Slovenije, 1971), p. 143.

[7] A story exploring the sexual behavior and psychology of a married woman, this novel bears a certain resemblance to heavy-hitters from other parts of Europe such as *Anna Karenina*, *Effi Briest*, *Madame Bovary*, and Borisav Stanković's *Bad Blood.*

some of Cankar's political speeches, so important in depicting the contexts of late Habsburg decline, the Great War, and the origins of Yugoslavia, are to be recommended to translators. The works discussed below would be on that list, as well as "Ni bilo v programu," ("It Wasn't on the Program") about systemic military violence, and "Ministerialna komisija" ("The Ministerial Commission") on Cankar's arrest and interrogation by Austrian authorities in 1914.

It might also be useful at this point to recommend some representative or especially thought-provoking works already available in English. The first *tranche* of new Cankar reading for the curious could well start with *The Ward of Our Lady of Mercy*. One could go on to include the following autobiographical works, for instance: "My Life," "The Fox," "Other Lives," "Our Plot," and "A Cup of Coffee."[8] They stress his profound love of nature in general and the Slovenian countryside in particular, the cruelty and exclusion inherent in human society, and his complex, adoring, and guilt-ridden relationship with his mother. Another set of stories that are indicative of Cankar's stylistic and thematic breadth are "The Shadows," "Verzdenec," "Local News Items," "Our Beautiful Country," and "The End."[9]

[8] All published in *My Life and Other Sketches*.

[9] All published in *Dream Visions and Other Selected Stories*. Translated and with a preface by Anton Druzina. Illustrated by Lillian Brulc. Willoughby Hills, OH: Slovenian Research Committee of America, 1982.

CANKAR'S NONFICTION

Cankar's life was crowded—not just with events in the personal and artistic realms but also with political engagement. He was a committed patriot and nationalist; he was also a committed advocate for the marginalized and vulnerable, the underdogs of society—or to use the words of a more ideologically explicit time than our own, the exploited or oppressed masses—who lived, or tried to, in thrall to poverty, disease, ignorance, hypocritical priests, and corrupt politicians. Of course these concerns come up, and often, in Cankar's literature. But they are also explicitly addressed in some of his speeches and essays. Most of these are unavailable in English; one sketch from late in his life, however, entitled "The Locked Chamber,"[10] conveys well his sense of political engagement and also his belief that his country stood at a crossroads in portentous times.

Cankar's famous speech "Slovenci in Jugoslavani" ("Slovenes and Yugoslavs," 1913) is a fascinating testimony to the power of South Slavic solidarity in the face of Habsburg callousness and growing international anarchy. Cankar is careful to state several times that Slovene culture, and especially language, should never be renounced or eroded, but that it makes great sense for Slovenes, Croats, and Serbs (and, presumably, Bosnians and even Bulgarians) to work together *politically.* Rather than any kind of assimilationist or capitulatory program, Cankar's message is actually one of dual emancipation

[10] In *My Life and Other Sketches*, pp. 180–183.

for Slovenes, one that stresses their subjectivity and agency: Slovenes should burst forth from the framework of unproductive and constrictive Habsburg political life at the same time they assert their cultural independence from both Serbs and Croats ("Illyrians")

Another very well known nonfiction item is "Kako sem postal socialist" ("How I Became a Socialist," 1913). Historians know quite well—even if today's politicians ignore the fact, and if popular culture has already forgotten it—that socialism has meant different things to different people at different times. More concretely we can safely assert that, before the enormities of Stalin's crimes became known, or before the centrally planned economies slowed down in the face of global energy issues and the demands of the service economy, socialism or communism was associated with the promise of radical change and also emitted the allure of certain key achievements. Personages as diverse as Milovan Djilas and Aleksandr Wat, for instance, attest to the former; the Five-year Plans, immunity to the Great Depression, the emancipation of women, resistance to racism and fascism (think Spanish Civil War! think Stalingrad!), and anti-colonial wars attest to the latter. Cankar, on the strength of his ethical concerns, fits into this category as well. He writes that after observing much "injustice, misery, evil, and hypocrisy,"[11] Cankar felt called to turn his attention to things more important than just poetry; he wanted to analyze "forces" and powers, not "dream

[11] In Boris Ziherl, ed. *Ivan Cankar in naš čas* (Ljubljana: Cankarjeva založba, 1976), p. 93.

of the stars."[12] Contemporary literature he condemned as "maudlin" and political parties as impotent, so he was drawn to the self-confidence, authenticity, and life-affirming programs of the socialists. It is very interesting to note as well that Cankar thought in global terms about economics and exploitation, in a way that was quite sophisticated for his day. He knew that Chinese laborers in the Transvaal were tearing up the earth to extract diamonds to be shown off by the ladies of New York; and this was just one example of what universally dominant capitalism meant: "the great masses of people are, by dint of their labor, the producers of culture, but not its consumers."[13] In addition, Cankar was an unorthodox and undogmatic socialist, and he asserted an early but unequivocal version of the right to what would be called by the 1940s "separate roads to socialism" for different countries.[14]

THIS BOOK

Martin Kačur was written in 1905 and published in early 1907 during Cankar's long stay in Vienna. It is the story of the decline and fall of an idealistic young teacher assigned to the Slovene hinterland. Kačur has already been

[12] *Ibid.*, p. 94.

[13] See "Slovensko ljudstvo in slovenska kultura," in Ivan Cankar, *Očiščenje in pomlajenje* (Ljubljana: Državna založba Slovenije, 1976), p. 34.

[14] See "Očiščenje in pomlajenje" in Ivan Cankar, *Očiščenje in pomlajenje* (Ljubljana: Državna založba Slovenije, 1976), p. 127.

assigned to Kotlina and then he moves to Zapolje, Blatni Dol,[15] and Lazi over the course of the book. Brilliant descriptions of Slovenia's natural beauty alternate with the haze of alcoholic despair, rural violence, marital alienation, and the death of a beloved young child. Young Kačur learns to compromise, quickly grows old, and feels keenly the rejection and hypocrisy of his colleagues. He finally meets his ruin fighting provincial prejudice and the cynicism of the ruling elites. He is much pained by his own inability to translate convictions into deeds; his failings as an activist, a pedagogue, and a husband are the subject of general mockery. But opportunism and betrayal on the part of others emerge as threats to his own well-being and to progress in general that are as potent as popular ignorance, bureaucracy, and the reactionary authorities' monopolies on force, wealth, and salvation. He is not well served by his friends Ferjan, Jerin, and Matilda, and after an unsuccessful courtship of the sexy Minka Sitar, he marries an enigmatically sensual and callous woman named Tončka. Their complex relationship produces three children, Tone, Francka, and little Lojze, to whom Kačur is very devoted but who dies as a toddler, precipitating the climactic personal and professional crises of the novel.

Kačur considers himself an "evangelist" of the betterment of his nation. He is on a mission to raise educa-

[15] Although not capitalized in Slovene, "dol" has been rendered "Dol" in this translation for the sake of clarity. One could also think of this town as "Muddyvale," a not inaccurate epithet produced by an exact translation.

tional standards and found reading circles and cultural societies to broaden people's horizons because he is a doctor to his nation, a savior-teacher, a poet of altruism. He will smite injustice and become a hero to the rescued vulnerable because, as he revels towards the end of the first chapter, "my calling is holy, as I myself am holy, and I will be consumed by its glory." But he ends up being consumed by other things, as he meets one heartless, unimaginative mayor, doctor, and priest after another and his projects collapse. His idealism, and then his health, submerge in barroom brawls, adultery, women's scorn, crowds of snickering children, and the shifting political terrain of operatives representing the Clericals, the Liberals, and various Germanophile, socialist, and anarchist ideas. Of course then the protagonist also ends up dealing with official investigations of his work resulting in reprimands and transfers. The occasional light-hearted tone employed by Cankar in early chapters still lets us know pretty clearly that Kačur's battle is an uphill one. We meet the flamboyantly anti-intellectual priest in shit-stained waders, gone rabidly "native" as a survival technique, and also the doctor in Zapolje with his prejudice against idealists who "plague humanity with love" and foolishness and "aid and abet charlatans disguising themselves as other crazy idealists to make it easier to steal gold and glory." But by the time Kačur laments, in the fifth chapter, that "[i]f Christ Himself could come to Blatni Dol, He'd hold His tongue," we know that the deep night and animalized population of rural Slovenia are anything but funny.

This novel is representative above all of Cankar's social realism and his political and economic critiques of fin-de-siècle society. Some of the emotional concerns of his other works, such as an innocent's quest for beauty and the idea of nature not as a refuge but a symbol of potential emotional fulfillment and the eventual happiness of a just society, are also present. No doubt a large part of the impact of *Martin Kačur* derives from Cankar's portrayal of the way society isolates people, denying them sympathy and solidarity; loneliness may be the ultimate helplessness, whether one is thinking in political, religious, or emotional terms. As Köstler has put it, for Cankar characters are often just "examples [or] facets of an all-encompassing anguish" [16] afflicting solitary or abandoned individuals. Cankar's style here owes a debt both to naturalism and to symbolism and also contains, in its sometimes frantic pace and associative interior monologues, hints of early expressionism.

When we think of representations of schoolteachers in popular and high culture, few correspondences to the eponymous protagonist in Cankar's *Martin Kačur* present themselves at first. Literature might seem of little help, actually, since what usually comes to mind first is the image of a martinet or a fuddy-duddy. Mr. Gradgrind, the headmaster in Charles Dickens' *Hard Times*, is a ready example; Arno Holz and Johannes Schlaf supply another, less well known European example in *Der erste Schultag* (1889). Turning to recent popular culture, we also see that

[16] See "Nachwort" in *Pavliček's Krone* (Klagenfurt/Celovec: Drava, 1995), p. 187.

films do not go very far towards helping us understand *Martin Kačur*, either, since Hollywood ultimately makes winners out of all the idealistic teachers with uphill battles, as in *Mr. Holland's Opus* (1995), *Freedom Writers* (2007), or, in less edifying (albeit endearing) fashion, in the 1970s television series *Welcome Back, Kotter.*

But a closer look at European and world literature of the past century and a half does gradually generate some correspondences to Cankar's setting in the novel at hand. If schoolteachers' lives are generally adjudged rather pedestrian and colorless, due either to the remoteness of their postings or the (supposedly) monk- or librarian-like introversion and tediousness rampant in their careers, they at least have the advantage of being necessary accompaniments to—if not agents of—modernization, necessary for everything from anchoring new ideologies (nationalism, communism) to improving lifestyles (industrialization, health and sanitation). It turns out that it is amazing what literacy can do! Cases for analysis and comparison can be found in Charlotte Brontë, *Jane Eyre*; Wilhelm Raabe, *Der Hungerpastor*; August Šenoa, *Branka*; Lazar Lazarević, "Školska ikona"; Ivo Andrić's essay "Učitelj Ljubomir"; Miroslav Krleža, *Povratak u Vučjak*; Branislav Nušic, *Analfabeta*; Ylljet Aliçka, "Parullat me gurë,"[17] John Fowles, *The Magus*; and in various works

[17] Available in English as "The Slogans in Stone," in Robert Elsie, ed., *Balkan Beauty, Balkan Blood: Modern Albanian Short Stories* (Evanston: Northwestern University Press, 2006), pp. 36–53. The story also served as the basis for the marvelous film *Slogans* (2001), directed by Gjergj Xhuvani.

by Yordan Yovkov and Maxim Gorky. Further parallels outside the European framework include Chinua Achebe, *A Man of the People*; Ngugi wa Thiongo, *The River Between*; Laura Ingalls Wilder, *These Happy Golden Years*; S. Alice Callahan, *Wynema: A Child of the Forest*; Edward Eggleston, *The Hoosier Schoolmaster*; Sinclair Lewis, *Main Street*; Max Braithwaite, *Why Shoot the Teacher?*; Sakae Tsuboi, *Twenty-four Eyes*; and Ernest Gaines, *A Lesson before Dying.*[18]

Slovene critics have exhibited a variety of opinions about *Martin Kačur.* France Bernik views it as the story of hope and love that miscarry in the face of ingratitude, resulting in the protagonist's "reconciliation with the swamp" of society around him.[19] There were many studies and conferences dedicated to Cankar's life and work during the decades of communist rule in Yugoslavia, and the writer was regularly lionized as an active champion of workers' rights and a herald of the coming socialist ascendancy; the highest-ranking Slovene politician, and President-for-life Tito's main theoretician, Edvard Kardelj, even went so far as to call Cankar a "prophet" of the anti-fascist war of national liberation (1941–1945)

[18] For other examples, see: Pamela Bolotin Joseph and Burnaford, Gail E. eds., *Images of Schoolteachers in Twentieth-Century America: Paragons, Polarities, Complexities* (NY: St Martins, 1994); Skinner, Hubert M., ed., *The Schoolmaster in Literature* (NY: American Book Company, 1892); and Fuess, Claude M. and Basford, Emory S., eds. *Unseen Harvests: A Treasury of Teaching* (NY: Macmillan, 1947).

[19] France Bernik, *Ivan Cankar: Ein slowenischer Schriftsteller des europäischen Symbolismus, 1876–1918* (München: Kovač, 1997), p. 164.

and subsequent Yugoslav federalism![20] Slightly less ecstatic is Dušan Moravec's assertion that *Martin Kačur* is "an unnerving ballad of a rebel born too soon."[21] Most ideological critiques of Cankar have tended to single out straightforward, explosive works like *The Bailiff Yerney* for praise, but all occasionally sounded an esthetic or psychological note as well when they commented on the yearning or passionate longing for justice evidenced by his characters. Sometimes the stress is on the futility of the Slovenes' struggles for national and socio-economic justice and *Martin Kačur's* mood of "sterility" and "gloom."[22] In Cankar's own day, the reception of *Martin Kačur* was mixed, as was the case with many of his works. Some critics faulted his pell-mell style, calling it sloppy; observers on the left sometimes found him too pessimistic (and later too religious) and observers on the right thought he was out of touch or cynical, if not subversive. One of the most intriguing assessments of Cankar, and of a number of his characters like Kačur, is that they were full of contradictions and attempted to solve social and literary problems "with the magic of bohemianism."[23] There was a film version of the novel

[20] See Kardelj, "Cankarjeva misel je danes enako živa" in *V areni življenja: ob stoletnici rojstva Ivana Cankarja* (Ljubljana: Komunist, 1977), p. 13.

[21] See Moravec, "Uvod," in Ivan Cankar, *Očiščenje in pomlajenje* (Ljubljana: Državna založba Slovenije, 1976), p. 8.

[22] See Lavrin, "Preface," in Ivan Cankar, *The Bishop Yerney and His Rights* (London: Pushkin Press, 1946), p. viii.

[23] Dušan Pirjevec, *Ivan Cankar in evropska literatura* (Ljubljana: Cankarjeva, 1964), p. 453.

made in the 1950s, and in 1983, the Triestine novelist Fulvio Tomizza transformed the book into a stage play called *The Idealist.* It is no surprise that the progressive intellectual Cankar produced other fiction dealing with teachers, as well: the short story "O čebelnjaku" (The Beehive) and the plays *Hlapci* (Farmhands), and *Pohujšanje v dolini šentflorjanski* (There's Something Rotten in the Valley of St. Florian).

CONCLUSION

Ivan Cankar was an outsider in his own day, and to a considerable degree he is an outsider in our day as well. But the reasons for his otherness—one need not say marginalization, for his works have already stood the test of time and are not in danger of sliding into oblivion—differ from the early 20th century to the early 21st. If Cankar pushed the envelope in his day for his depictions of eroticism, abuse, and despair, and suffered censorship for it, and if his outspoken political views earned him a jail cell in the authoritarian Habsburg Empire during the First World War, we can easily forgive him for those things today. What seems quaint or mystifying about him today is that he believed in socialism (chuckle!) or even Yugoslavism (gasp!); furthermore, that useless old crutch of literary criticism about "local" versus "universal" values and themes prevents many an enthusiastic reader from enjoying works from other parts of the world. Just because a novel contains proper nouns from other languages and realia from other places does not mean it is an obscure "ethnographic" project that deserves to be consigned to shelves of dusty academic works. Too often we forget that false distinctions between local and universal, or the historic and the timeless, are really based on intellectual indolence and the unthinking absorption into one's own moment.

There are, I would argue, three Ivan Cankars. The first is the iconic representative of Slovene modernism, the oft-studied and highly praised movement known as the *Moderna.* If there was any doubt left (after Prešeren in the mid-19th century, or even after the Protestant Reformation three hundred years earlier) about whether Slovene intellectuals and artists could "run with the big dogs"—mingle and cross-pollinate with pan-European trends, about whether this small rural Central European (or even Balkan?) people could embrace the cosmopolitan and industrial world of Vienna and beyond, it was dispelled by Cankar's voluminous success. Much is made about the modernism of Cankar's writing. This is not due to his political views or use of the satirical and grotesque. Rather, it is partly due to the styles he embraced in his various phases: naturalism, decadence, psychological realism, and symbolism. He eventually even flirts with expressionism, with its wild oral delivery and description, starkly contrasting scenes, and flashbacks. The other modern aspect of Cankar's writing is his use of language—imbuing Slovene with a new melody and rhythm, a more agile and poetic sensibility, while also using folk elements to great advantage.

The second, iconoclastic, Cankar often hides in the shadows today. He is Cankar the radical. We can stomach this Cankar (the "bad boy") pretty easily today, though we need historians to remind us of the importance of context in appreciating his political concerns.

The third Cankar is the artist, the word painter, the restless, chaotic, angry, sometimes graphic, but in the last analysis very human and humane writer whose personality and life hover close to his texts. From his pen onto the page, flying below the radar of ideological litmus tests, comes an explosive flow of events and personalities that have the power to infect the reader and rouse him or her to action. Cankar has the drive of an expressionist, the heart of a Romantic, the pantheistic abstractions of a symbolist, and the tool-kit of a naturalist.

Towards the end of his life, amidst a lengthy artistic phase that was once again heavily symbolist, though now with a spiritual rather than sensual coloration, Cankar penned an impassioned *cri de coeur* about the writer's mission entitled "A View from the Casket."[24] This sketch is a vehement reassertion of political consciousness and commitment; a writer is supposed to be very much in the world even if he or she is very much against that world. The mayhem of the first total war and its dying empires produces the dramatic phrasing: when "universal injustice" and "universal death" blast the world, which side are you on? Cankar's response is crystal clear: envy, fear, indolence, counterfeit beauty, squeamishness—none of this should keep writers from their mission. Alas, Martin Kačur himself lacked this

[24] In *My Life and Other Sketches*, pp. 159–162.

passion and discipline, but the author of *Martin Kačur* had it right up till the end of his truncated life.

Some critics have dismissed Cankar's *engagement* as "early impressionistic extravagances"[25] or as "fruitless sensualism and moral relativism."[26] But Cankar was aware of the great demands of his radically changing epoch: "If you are too weak in these times of horror, might, and struggle" he wrote, "lock yourself up and rot. You will be no great loss."[27] Cankar's early death was of course a great loss. But even the weakness and failure of Kačur the man did more than demonstrate the literary accomplishment of our author; Kačur and Cankar together reveal both the power of the obscurantist agenda and the fragility of human happiness.

[25] See Lavrin, p. xi "Preface" in Ivan Cankar, *The Bishop Yerney and His Rights* (London: Pushkin Press, 1946), p. xi.

[26] See Irena Avsenik Nabergoj, *Mirror of Reality and Dreams: Stories and Confessions by Ivan Cankar* (Frankfurt am Main: Peter Lang, 2008), p. 24.

[27] Cankar, *My Life and Other Sketches*, p. 162.

BIBLIOGRAPHY

Translations of Cankar's works into English:[28]

The Bailiff Yerney and His Rights. Translated by Sidonie Yeras and H.C. Sewell Grant. Introduction by Janko Lavrin. Illustrated by Nora Lavrin. London: Pushkin Press, 1930.

"Children and Old Folk," translated by Helen Hlacha, in Hiram Haydn and John Cournos, eds., *A World of Great Stories* (New York: Crown Publishers, 1947), pp. 709–711.

Dream Visions and Other Selected Stories. Translated and with a preface by Anton Druzina. Illustrated by Lillian Brulc. Willoughby Hills, OH: Slovenian Research Committee of America, 1982.

My Life and Other Sketches. Selected and Introduced by Josip Vidmar. Translated by Elza Jereb and Alasdair MacKinnon. Ljubljana: Državna založba Slovenije, 1971.

"Prešce," translated by David Limon, in *Slovene Studies: The Journal of the Society for Slovene Studies* 5:2 (1983), 219–232.

The Ward of Our Lady of Mercy. Translated by Henry Leeming. Introduction by Anton Slodnjak. Ljubljana: Državna založba Slovenije, 1976.

[28] For a complete listing of individual items by Cankar now in English translation, see Vasa D. Mihailovich, *A Comprehensive Bibliography of Yugoslav Literature in English, 1593–1980* (Columbus: Slavica, 1984), and its three supplements going up to 1998.

Critical works on Cankar in English: [29]

Avsenik Nabergoj, Irena. *Mirror of Reality and Dreams: Stories and Confessions by Ivan Cankar.* Translated by Jason Blake. Frankfurt am Main: Peter Lang, 2008.

Herrity, Peter. "Poems of the Slovene *Moderna*." In Cynthia Marsh and Wendy Rosslyn, eds., *Russian and Yugoslav Culture in the Age of Modernism* (Nottingham: Astra Press, 1991), pp. 123–132.

Kocijancic, Nike. "On Louis Adamic's Translation of Cankar's Jernej's Justice." In *Slovene Studies: The Journal of the Society for Slovene Studies* 15:1–2 (1993), 139–150.

Lavrin, Janko. "The Conscience of a Small Nation (On Ivan Cankar)," in his *Aspects of Modernism* (London: Nott, 1935), pp. 197–207.

Ozbalt, Irma M. "Emigrants in Ivan Cankar's Fiction." In *Slovene Studies: The Journal of the Society for Slovene Studies* 4:2 (1982), 99–112.

———. "Ivan Cankar." In Vasa D. Mihailovich, ed., *South Slavic Writers before World War II* (Detroit: Gale Research, 1995), pp. 24–32.

Slodnjak, Anton. "Ivan Cankar in Slovene and World Literature." In *Slavonic and East European Review* 59 (April 1981): 186–196.

Zdovc, Sonja. "The Use of Novelistic Techniques in Slovene Journalism." In *Journalism Studies* 18:2 (2007): pp. 248–263.

[29] Cankar's translated works of fiction also contain useful introductory essays.

PART I

CHAPTER ONE

Mudstained and damp with dew, Martin Kačur walked into the small restaurant attached to the post courier's station.

"Does the coach to Zapolje leave soon?"

"Yes, soon! In half an hour," answered the sleepy-eyed tavern-keeper.

Kačur took a seat at the table and ordered brandy and bread. He tossed the large bundle from his thick staff onto the bench.

His ruddy, robust face brimmed with the freshness of an autumn morning, as did his moist, merry eyes. He already had a lengthy pilgrimage behind him, two tough hours; and a whiff of pungent fog and black dawn still clung to his cheeks and clothes.

A stout, elderly man came banging into the tavern. It was only September, but already he wore a long, heavy sheepskin coat and a black fur cap. He was heavy-jowled and unshaven; he looked out irritably from under eyebrows that were bushy and gray with age. The proprietor greeted him with pronounced deference and brought him brandy, ham, and bread.

"What? Jernej still isn't here?"

"He's already been in. But then he left for the post office."

The heavy-set man drank and ate and glanced over at Kačur. He studied his face thoroughly, sized up his clothing, and realized that Kačur was a respectable sort of person.

"Where are you headed?"

"To Zapolje."

"And what will your job be there?"

"Teacher."

"Hm."

He took an even closer look at Kačur, and if the latter's eyes had not been misty from the dew, he would have recognized both compassion and *schadenfreude* in the portly gentleman's gaze.

"I'm from Zapolje, too!" announced the fat man, digging around in his mouth with a toothpick. "I am the doctor there. An accursed backwater—there's no place worse on the planet! But I'm not saying anything! It's a pretty region; if only those people weren't there!"

Kačur smiled.

"Everybody says things like that. I do, too, when I'm talking about my hometown. I say: 'Lovely, and if only there were no people there!' And yet those people are meek and timid, good and deserving of respect. All people are good!"

The doctor flung his toothpick to the floor, propped his elbows up on the table and gave him a nasty look.

"So this is what we're in for?"

"How's that?" asked Kačur with a sense of alarm.

"A blockhead like you? No offense intended.—All people are good? You'll soon see how good they are!—There's not a human being on this earth who is good, including you and me! But what am I saying?—I'll say this to you straight out, because you're a decent young man: be absolutely, positively, completely careful and absolutely, positively, completely hypocritical when you get to Zapolje. That's all I can tell you."

God only knows what all he's experienced, thought Kačur, and the fat doctor started to intrigue him.

"Now, friend, you just gave me the sort of look that young people of today always give us older folks: 'He doesn't understand people anymore, and he doesn't know what times are like.' However, my boy, that's not it.—Some schnaps, Jurij!—That's not the case. Can you imagine that ten years ago I was still a big speaker at the rallies?[1] That I was fighting for our national rights? That I was on the watch list of the political police? No go? Of course not! I'm fat! But I tell you what: in that town you will see people who are even more easy-going than I am, and lazier, people who are a lot fatter than I and who've never been written up in the police files. People who no Habsburg[2] loyalists look askance at and who nonetheless—Lord have mercy!—are meritorious and eminent patriots! They weren't at the rallies; they were hanging

[1] A reference to *narodni tabori*, mass meetings in the Slovene countryside, held in the late 1860s, which demonstrated support for early Slovene nationalist agendas and celebrated folk culture

[2] In Cankar's text the term is "imperial and royal," the Slovene equivalent of the inimitable Austrian phrase *kaiserlich-königlich*, or "*k. und k.*"

around in government offices, and yet nowadays you have to raise your hat to them, if you please."

The doctor launched a heavy wad of spit into the middle of the room. Kačur smiled inside, amused: look at that, the old-fashioned patriotism of the mass meetings, naïve and selfless.

"And yet, sir, you've stayed put there!"

The doctor gave him an exasperated look.

"So where else am I supposed to be? What, do you think it's better anywhere else? If a person has to live in manure, then it's best for him always to live in the same manure; all manure stinks, after all, but most of all at the start. Later you get accustomed to it!"

He's been through a lot, thought Kačur. He almost felt sorry for the doctor.

"You are still young. You want to begin your service.—But is Zapolje your first posting?"

"My second. Earlier I was in Kotlina, but I had a falling out with the mayor and he pushed me out. I don't regret it. Kotlina was truly a pit."[3]

"So! You quarreled with the mayor.—Well, there we have it: you're still young and you could stand to learn a few more lessons. Therefore I will tell you this, and remember it well, if you wish to live in peace in Zapolje and with people everywhere: don't quarrel with anyone, ever, and if someone asserts that donkeys have green fur, then let your response be: yes, and how green it is!—

[3] One of Cankar's rare puns, and an even rarer one that works in English. The name of the town, Kotlina, means basin or hollow in Slovene.

And what's more, don't stick your nose where it doesn't belong. Over there in Kotlina, did you raise the civilizational level of the population?"

"I was trying to." Kačur went red in the face. "That's why I had this conflict with the mayor. And with the parish priest, too."

"Then you already know from experience that educating the populace is not a sound or worthwhile enterprise. Therefore, refrain from doing that, and avoid it especially in Zapolje, because the people there are more in need of instruction than anywhere else and you could be sorely tempted and easily seduced. It is dangerous to fall out of favor with the mayor and even more dangerous with the priest. Offend God and He'll forgive you; offend a priest and they'll give you a transfer! So leave the people alone. Will you be getting married?"

"No!" Kačur was astounded. Listening to the doctor made him feel like he was standing under a cloudburst.

"Don't ever marry, and, as a matter of fact, steer clear of women insofar as you can, because you are a teacher. Experiences with women leave even an ordinary man like myself embittered.—That is to say, I am married.—But for a teacher who gets married the best thing would be for him to hang a millstone around his own neck and drown himself in the depths of the sea. Accordingly: don't ever get married.—Are you a singer?"

"I am."

"Don't ever sing out loud. Except in church. But don't sing too loudly even there, lest the folks in Zapolje call you a braggart. Don't ever sing in the tavern, or they'll claim that you're a drunkard. And don't sing in a group, for they will say that you're trying to stir people up. Not in your room either, because that will mean you're an idiot. Don't go out too much, or else they'll consider you shiftless and trivial, but also don't keep to yourself too much, because then they'll say you're sneaky.—Do you have any political convictions?"

"I do."

"Bury them in the most remote corner of your heart!—For a lie is a sin only when it's useless. If you can choose between lying and telling the truth, and the difference doesn't cost you much, then opt for the truth, because then it will be all the easier for you to tell lies when you need them. Don't be obstinate, especially with political convictions. When you deem it advantageous to change those convictions, quote *Tugomer*[4]: 'Be tough....', etc.—And no one will notice the change. But if anyone should happen to discover your second countenance, then say that you are evolving in the spirit of the times. And if they then reproach you for flip-flopping or being an opportunist or a swindler, answer thus: griping is easy but doing is hard! And remember: nobody is working just for himself or herself—but everybody is working for the good of the people! Be respectful of the convictions of your neighbor, for it could someday be of use to you. Do you write poetry?"

"Yes, I've written some of that, too," Kačur answered, staring at the table.

[4] The name of a (probably mythical) tragic Slovene national hero from the 10th century, popularized in dramas by Josip Jurčič (1844–1881) and Fran Levstik (1831–1887).

"Don't do it; it will cost you credibility. And since we're on the topic of poems, we need to speak of drinking, too. Don't think you have to drink just because you're a patriot. Sober men have also become members of parliament. Will you keep all my advice in mind?"

"I will," Kačur smiled.

"And even if you commit all this to memory, and act accordingly, you'll still have a difficult enough time in this life. God Himself could go out among the people, especially among the Zapoljans, and get nowhere with them. If nothing else, they'd hold His divinity against Him."

Is he being serious, or is this a joke? Kačur pondered. He's bitter, and God only knows what all he's seen. He's not a malicious man, and he also can't be unhappy. He's too fat for that, and he enjoys food too much.

"All aboard!" the coachman yelled into the tavern. He was a tall, bony old man with a red nose.

"This is our new teacher," said the doctor as he introduced Kačur. The postilion was looking at him from the side and sized him up with a quick, stern look.

"He's still young, sir. Plus he's small! I've always said that a teacher can't afford to be either young or small."

The doctor and the teacher got into the carriage. It was small and low and crammed with boxes and parcels. The coachman cracked the whip behind the horses and the carriage began to rock and creak. Kačur opened the window and looked cheerfully out at the dew-drenched landscape of morning.

The road twisted its way along steep, forested heights. To the right, a plain spread into the distance; long wisps of fog, veil-like, lazily worked their way across it. Occasionally the fog split open and the fields came gleaming through. Now and then a tall poplar would pop out of the middle of the smooth plain and then be submerged again immediately in fog. A village would appear on the road, just two or three houses together; to Kačur they seemed unusually white and festive.

"I've never seen such beautiful villages before. The houses are sparkling as if it were Sunday, with the sun shining and the bells tolling for vespers!"

The doctor had an expression of annoyance on his face.

"You should have another look at them in a month or two. They'll be as filthy as everything else on the planet!"

"May God forgive him for all that pessimism!" Kačur smiled to himself. "If I were a superstitious man, I would have to believe that He had sent you into my path Himself as an ill omen."

The carriage moved past an old castle. It was surrounded by a large garden with a rushing brook. Foaming and splashing, it poured out from under the tall boulders above the road. Close by stood an open gazebo under a spreading chestnut tree. It had ivy covering its windows and dangling above the door. A young girl in a red blouse was sitting in the gazebo. She turned around, and for a moment Kačur saw, as if in the briefest of dreams, a white face and two large, black eyes. From the medieval castle a flock of screeching birds rose into the air, and the carriage swayed on, as a broad, unencumbered plain opened up before it.

Kačur sighed.

"This is Bistra," announced the doctor. "A person might almost say that it's an attractive little village. But if you don't want to get hitched—and I've already told you that you shouldn't do that—then don't even come visit here!"

"Are there many pretty girls here then?"

"Yes. An awful lot of them!"

Kačur thought of the old castle, the open gazebo, the ivy, and the red blouse, and he was deeply moved.

The carriage turned onto the bright surface of a broad lane. Peaceful green water, half-concealed under old willows, lay right beside the road. The sun shone forth from behind the fog and, on the far side of the river, at the foot of a far-away hill, Zapolje gleamed in colorful, fresh splendor. A small city, akin to a village, climbed up out of the fields off the plain and onto the gently rising hills, while up high, looming large under the sky, great forests in a colossal half-circle stared mutely down at the flatlands.

"There's Zapolje!" said the doctor, looking out at it indifferently and pointing with his little finger.

Kačur said nothing. He was dumbfounded by what he saw. The beauty detected by his eyes lifted his thoughts—which were already lofty and gay—to the level of the heavens. He trembled in festive anticipation. He felt the force growing within him; he felt life welling up, booming and blooming, rushing riotously into the future.

The fat doctor looked at his flushed cheeks and his feverish eyes, and he laid a hand on his shoulder.

"Don't be angry with me, young man, if my teachings were a bit simplistic. But believe me, I meant well, and it would do you no harm to act accordingly. Yet I already know—I can see it on your face—that you won't be following my advice. Therefore I say: take care of yourself, first and foremost and always. The other folks will fend for themselves! And if you are of the opinion that you absolutely must help your neighbor, then do so without making a big fuss, without all that solemnity; that way, it will do you less harm! Last night, at midnight, droopy-eyed and stuffed-up from this head cold, I drove to Rakitna in some dreadful little chaise to treat a woman there, a cottager, who had very suddenly taken ill. At the halfway point, at the top of a bluff, the chaise broke down, and I had to rove from inn to inn, and now I'm riding home with the postal courier. I am only telling you this because I couldn't tell anybody else; it would mean forfeiting some of my dignity and respect. I also used to go around to the demonstrations, my friend, and speak of the rights of the Slovenian people. But I was younger then, and now I know that all that activity was of no use to me or to others, even less than this trip I'm on today.—Well, here we are at home, good sir! If you have any problems, you can turn to me. I'll be happy to see you!"

The carriage halted in front of the station-house inn, a new two-storey building that gleamed with whitewash. Across the street stood the old post office; it was a dark and uninviting structure. A stream coursed past the post office, calm and broad, with willows drooping into it. The doctor shook Kačur's hand and strode off with heavy, resounding steps. He was tall and broad in the shoulder but walked a bit bent over.

Kačur entered the tavern. He took a seat at the window and looked up the street, across the market up to the light-colored little church that stood gleaming at the foot of the slope. At the top there were sun-splashed heights and young trees, still very green; and yet another church, white and resplendent in the morning sunshine. He watched people walking past in the street: civil servants, peasants, laborers. It seemed to him that they would all be amiable and pleasant to live with, since he saw no repulsive or ill-humored faces.

"Now is when my real life starts!" he thought. "Now is when I have to act on all that I've been planning."

He was in a solemn mood, and the thought occurred to him that his heart was as pure and full of hope as at his first communion.

"And in the name of God," he started to say out loud. He was no longer thinking of the fat doctor or his precepts.

"Do you have a room to let?" he asked the rotund wife of the tavern-keeper.

"We do have one, sir," she said. "But, Jesus and Mary, just yesterday evening a lady arrived from Trieste. She's pretty, and the way she dresses! My Lord! You will see her directly, when she comes through the entrance hall. And a gentleman arrived after her as well. God only knows where he's from. Nobody here knows him."

"And what about that room?

"We do have one more. But our Tone sleeps there whenever he comes home."

"Could you let me have it for one day?

"We can certainly do that. Tone only comes here once a year for three days."

Kačur left, untied his bundle, washed up, and changed his clothes.

The room was large and empty; four wide windows looked in. In the corner stood a bed, glum and lonely as if in a cemetery. A stream flowed past outside, quiet and broad like a pond, and in the distance dark forests gaped.

"A nice punishment!" Kačur laughed. "From fetid Kotlina into this sunlight! Of course there I was the master, the emperor in my school, and they say that here I'll be just a hired hand. Nonetheless sun is sun, and you're only a servant if you put up with it."

He regarded himself in the mirror: the requisite hair-style, black necktie, black coat, black trousers.

"And now—off to the dignitaries, to the patriots!"

He smiled, but his insides were not completely at ease, and instead of leaving immediately he waited in the tavern, partaking of spirits. He was thinking about the fat doctor.

"Did they have to place this rotund omen in my path, this discouragement in my heart? Instead of thinking about my great mission, I feel like a servant already!"

He stood up, in a foul mood, and headed out. The fog had already burnt off, and the warm autumnal sun, affable and jolly, welcomed him by lingering on his countenance.

"Look at this! And to think I was almost melancholy!" Now Kačur smiled. "Okay, there's the big general store, and the mayor's probably in there."

He went into the foyer, and a heavyset man with thin legs, a red face, and a goatee came towards him. He wore hunting-garb and danced about with strange little leaps.

"What'll it be?" he said hurriedly, in a voice that was at once lively, squeaky, and bouncy. "What'll it be? Good day! What can I do for you? Greetings! Where are you from? Come in! Over there, over there—who are you?"

Martin Kačur was perplexed. He went through a door he had not noticed before and sat down at a table where two glasses stood next to a bottle of wine. He sat down but got up again immediately and bowed.

"My name is Martin Kačur. I've been named the new teacher in Zapolje and I wish to pay my respects to the mayor of the town."

"That would be me, sir. The mayor of Zapolje is—none other than I!"

And he laughed merrily. As he bounced and pranced around, he shook Kačur's hand, patted him on the shoulder, and pressed him down onto a chair.

"Would you like something to drink? Would you?"

And he poured him a glass.

"Have you already been to anyone else's office?"

"No, not at anybody's."

"For real?"

"Yes."

"You're lying!"

The mayor winked, crossed his arms over his stomach, and laughed at the top of his lungs.

"I have only just arrived," Kačur explained earnestly and with a touch of irritation. "I have not spoken with a single person from Zapolje, save the doctor."

"The doctor?" asked the mayor, now overwrought. He was leaning far over the table. "What did he say? Did he say anything about me? Just tell me!"

"He didn't say anything." Kačur was astonished. "What could he have said?"

"So he did! I know he told you something about me! You just don't want to say it, that's all! Oh—for Pete's sake!"

He stared at Kačur, roared with laughter once more, and then broke off abruptly and became serious again.

"So, now! So now you are one of us. I hope you will do everything in your power—well, you know. One must educate the youth in a spirit of belief and—well, you know! Are you a member of the National Party?"[5]

"I am!"

"Hm. I'm one, too. But—one mustn't overdo anything. Thriftiness—a wonderful virtue. If you exaggerate it—then it's avarice. A sin!—*Können Sie deutsch*?[6]

"I can."

"*Kann ich.*[7]—Good! The children should learn only German. What's with all that other stuff? What is a farmer supposed to do with it? Now, education and progress are all well and good. But we understand each other, eh?"

[5] The National Progressive Party, or *Narodna napredna stranka*, also known as the Liberals. This parliamentary grouping, and eventual political party, hewed to a modern political line, recognizable in many other parties around Europe in the 1890s: nationalistic, constitutionalist, and usually urban, middle-class and secular. In Cankar's work, a member of this party is called a *narodnjak*.

[6] Can you speak German? (German in the original.)

[7] I can. (German in the original.)

Suddenly the earnestness disappeared from his face and he burst out in merry laughter. Kačur blushed and felt as though he'd been smoking strong tobacco or drinking heavy wine. He got to his feet and stretched out an unsteady hand for his hat.

"Well? Where to? Where to? Where are you off to now? To the priest? That will be quite an experience! You'll see that he's rather a piece of work! But we're friends, the priest and I, and therefore I'll say nothing about it. Just go see him, and you'll see for yourself.—Why didn't you finish the wine? It's good wine. I mean, you know—a man can have a drink at home, or in the pub..."

And the mayor clutched his belly with both hands and laughed resoundingly. His red goatee jiggled as he winked with his red eyes.

"Whoa, there—one more thing."

He took Kačur by the hand and pulled him into the foyer.

"Be straight with me! Are you with the Clericals?[8]

"Me?" Kačur responded, amazed.

"So you are? Huh?"

"No. I don't concern myself with such things."

He tore his hand free. Fire bloomed across his cheeks.

The mayor bent slightly forward at the waist, smiled, and gave a roguish wink.

[8] The Slovene People's Party, or *Slovenska ljudska stranka*, also founded in the 1890s. In Cankar's work, a member of this party is called a *klerikalec*, and an adjective used to describe the party is *farški*, as in German *Pfarrer* or the English parish.

"Of course not! Not in any way, shape, or form! Nowadays nobody really knows how it will all turn out. Hence it's always a good thing to avoid siding with one or the other. These are nasty times, to be sure!—But off you go now, for God's sake!"

He shook Kačur's hand warmly and then drew so close that he could have kissed the other man's face. And then he leapt backwards, as if he had changed his mind about something. Then the door clicked shut behind Kačur, and he was standing on the street with his face still flushed.

"The tubby doctor knows that guy," Kačur mused. He walked on, lost in thought. His head was lowered, but the sun was beaming, the housed gleamed like at Easter, and the mists had lifted.

"So what was our mayor like back there in Kotlina?" Kačur pondered. "He was a nitwit. This one is not a nitwit at least, although he is in other respects an odd bird. Well, God bless him!"

He began walking along the broad, white road that wound in a great curve higher and higher up the slope to where the parish church stood. He strode along as if he were on the path to freedom. The sky seemed higher and higher to him, and ever more clear, while below him the colorful fields stretched ever further. Zapolje gleamed at his feet.

He shouted out in a robust voice: "There is no compulsion!...One doesn't have to fear other people, or obey them! Or follow their lead! Behave like the earth; do as the fields do! Bear fruit whenever you wish to! Humans are their slaves! This is how it should be: I am my own man! I'm free! A voluntary servitor to all!"

Part I: Chapter One

The tall white rectory flashed into view next to the parish building. Martin Kačur walked calmly onto the grounds. He went up some stairs and rang the bell.

"Who's there?" asked a deep, gruff voice from behind the glass door.

"At least you know where you stand with him," thought Kačur to himself, and he rang a second time.

An exasperated arm pulled the door open, and Kačur caught sight of a short, heavy-set older man in a long gown.

Kačur bowed. "Martin Kačur, the teacher!"

The priest looked him up and down, silently, for a long time with eyes that were cold and inexpressive. He then gave Kačur's hand a perfunctory shake.

"I know, I know," he said slowly, neither affably nor rudely. "No one has said anything bad about you, but there's been nothing good either. *Tabula rasa.*—Well, come inside for a bit."

In a sleepy voice he beckoned to Kačur and led him slowly into a large room. A long table stood in the middle; the walls were bare, except for a miserable black crucifix hanging in one corner.

"This certainly isn't the place where he receives guests of the better sort," thought Kačur, as he sat down across from the cleric. He twirled his hat on his knees and grew more and more ill at ease. The blood ran to his head, and when he noticed that he was blushing, he blushed even more.

"I think," the priest said in that same testy, sleepy voice, "I think that we will understand each other and that you'll be with us for a long time. But I will tell you flat out that I have no confidence in the younger generation. They rave over ideas they do not understand and cannot process, and when they grow confused, they ultimately create confusion in the whole populace. I knew immediately where these enthusiastic mass meetings would lead, with their exaggerated sense of nationalism...Well, we'll talk about this more later. They wanted to force this flake Arko on us; you probably know him, that rabble-rouser. But he wouldn't have lasted two weeks with us, I can assure you, and I assured them. As far as you are concerned, we have learned that in...—Where were you exactly? In Kotlina!—You were up to something. But as I said: you are still young, a blank slate, and we shall see what you inscribe upon it!"

The priest arose and shook his hand as coolly and loosely as when he had first greeted him.

"That does not bode well!" Kačur smiled mournfully to himself as he left the presbytery. "He's a quiet man, but tough. Hard! Then again, I won't be having any contact with him. I regret stopping by to see him."

On the far side of the church building, across from the house of the curate, stood the school: it was an old, gray building. The house of the curate was equally unwelcoming, and dark, but behind it a shady garden extended down the road. And in that garden a young, rosy-cheeked man with a breviary in his hand was strolling along a pleasant, sandy path.

With quiet envy, Kačur beheld the garden, and the gazebo hidden behind some trees, and the rosy-cheeked curate. Then he looked back at the school, which now seemed even more deserted and grim.

"No joy will materialize from out of those doors," he said to himself. The thought made him shiver, and he walked dejectedly on up the slope.

At the top of the grade, amidst a small garden, stood a one-story house with green windows. It was surrounded by a wooden fence painted red. A dazzling white wall was visible under the grapevines that spiraled up to the roof.

"This must be it, according to the directions I got.—He's got it good here!"

Seated on a bench in front of the house was a strapping, big-bellied man; he wore no jacket but had on a snow-white, long-sleeved shirt with gold cufflinks that gleamed at his wrists. On top of his black vest a long golden chain was draped; his trousers were impeccably ironed and the shoes shone like a mirror, with not a speck of dust to be seen on them. The portly man's face was uncommonly mild, pale, and heavy-jowled, with peaceful, philanthropic eyes peering out from behind gilt-framed glasses.

Kačur gave a greeting, and the man stood up; he extended both his arms and his face radiated enormous kindness.

"Mr. Headmaster, sir, please allow me to introduce myself—"

"Aha, our new faculty member! I knew it right when I saw you coming up the incline. A warm, warm welcome to you! I'm already convinced that we will hit it off fine, that we will get along exquisitely."

Kačur noticed that the teacher spoke a very pure Slovene. His pronunciation followed the orthography exactly; he didn't leave off a single ending, and neither in his pronunciation nor the rhythm of his speech was there any trace of dialect.

"And they told me he's from Ribnica!" thought Kačur. "But he's straight out of a book, the grammar book!"

The sweetness and congeniality did not suit Kačur in the least, and he would have much preferred for the teacher to be a loud, peevish, and imperious man instead.

"Have you already had a look around Zapolje?"

"On the trip here I talked some with the doctor, and I've already paid a visit to the mayor and the priest."

The headmaster smiled and gently wagged his index finger at him.

"Before anything else, you're supposed to introduce yourself to your superior!—But of course I'm just pulling your leg. I'm not your boss, but rather your colleague and friend. Have you seen the school yet?"

"Yes, I have. For a town as pretty and as sizable as this one, the building seems pretty old and dreary to me."

"Don't judge a book by its cover! What you call age and dreariness is more appropriate for a school than shine and boastfulness. You are aware of the fact that we must instill in the youth a sense of seriousness and humility. People study better in dark rooms than bright ones. Plus, young people are more even-tempered in the rain than in the sun!"

Kačur did not respond. The cloying, calm, earnest demeanor of the headmaster was suffocating him. It lay like a thick, cold shadow above his eyes and over his heart. The headmaster shook his right hand as he placed his left on Kačur's shoulder.

"Well, now, my friend! We'll be getting to know each other much better, because there's nobody you know better than a colleague from the workplace!"

Kačur made a silent bow and left. He felt his throat closing up, and his eyes grew so cloudy they could barely take in a fraction of the beauty lying far beneath him on the broad, sunny plain.

"But how could it be any different? Or why should it be?" he pondered. "Of what have I grown afraid? Everything you aren't ordered to do is prohibited and contravenes the laws of this society. What, was I supposed to believe that things would change from one day to the next? Soft loam is easy to till, but a field of stone makes for hard plowing."

He turned off the road and followed a steep path to a hollow that was hidden under high, perpendicular rock walls. Up above, the green trees peered down into the darkness; the glen was murky and cold, and a stream flowed out of the boulders; from its very source it was dark green, broad, and placid. A path wound its way up the high rock wall; a wooden footbridge had been laid across the creek and a bench hewn into the stone.

Kačur sat down. The stillness around him grew even deeper as soon as his footsteps could no longer be heard in the sand. The water was tranquil, as if it were under a spell turning it into a sheet of diaphanous stone. The willows stood motionless, staring noiselessly at their black reflections traced onto the green looking-glass; and not a single ray of sunshine strayed into the gorge.

Far behind him, as if in a large window, Zapolje was gleaming in the splendor of midday. Bells tolled in the parish church and the dull, half-muffled sound ricocheted off the gray walls without breaking the stillness.

Kačur sighed deeply, as if he were unshouldering a great burden. He felt freer and more powerful in the wilderness; the things he had experienced seemed smaller and less significant. From a distance he turned his contented eyes on the people who had been standing in front of him a short while before; he could now view them more probingly and draw more sober conclusions about them.

"That greatest of all faults is missing from every one of them. None of them has firm views, ideas, convictions—that's why there's nobody to fight against; no one has a weapon. These are tired people, forlorn and sullen from their ceaseless, unvarying, and insipid labor. Deep in their hearts, they are people like any others, good and honest. It's just that you have to get used to them, bear in mind their hardships and their poverty. A machine is only dangerous as long as you don't understand how it operates."

When he left the gorge for the road, his step was lighter. Women came towards him, carrying lunches to the brick factory. A well-dressed, thin, sallow-faced man, probably an official, went past, looking at him with curiosity and mistrust, while down below in the field a long row of women with colorful kerchiefs and sickles in their hands moved down the furrows and then sat down in the grass along the path. The air, which had been clean and fresh, was filled with dusty, hot stickiness, and the sun came baking down as if it were August.

Kačur felt fatigued when he entered the inn. After lunch he went out to find lodging in the vicinity of the presbytery. It ended up being a cramped room with tatty, old-fashioned furniture.

"This is also where the previous teacher lived," the landlady, who was the wife of the merchant, revealed.

"Was he in Zapolje long?"

"No, barely a year. He disappeared overnight. Nobody stays here very long."

"Why did he leave?"

"He fraternized with the workers and didn't go to mass. He was a good man, but he didn't know how to behave properly."

Kačur made arrangements with the woman for his meals. In his mind he calculated that he would have five florins per month left over for pocket-money.

That first night he slept in the inn, in a large, empty room. He breathed easier once he had blown out the light. And once he had blown out the light, the dull rushing sound started underneath the window, so he got up and closed it.

"By day the water didn't hiss like that. It lay as still as a pool. It must only wake up at night," he thought.

The faces he had met during the day filed past in his mind. And when he had fallen asleep, he saw himself standing in the priest's large, bright chamber, pounding on the table with his fist until the breviary dropped off the side.

"I made a commitment to live and breathe for my nation, and there is no power that can hold me back! My calling is holy, as I myself am holy, and I will be consumed by its glory..."

He threw off his blanket and then awoke in a foul mood. The four windows, large and dark, stared in at him; the stream rustled below.

He closed his eyes, but he had not yet fallen asleep when his thoughts set out in a brighter direction. He saw the castle, old and gray and surrounded by an extensive park; he saw the gazebo by the road, cloaked in ivy; and in the gazebo he saw the gleaming red blouse and a fair face with black eyes.

He sighed and smiled in his half-slumber.

CHAPTER TWO

It was on a Sunday morning, deep in November, that Martin Kačur made the pilgrimage from Zapolje to Bistra. The sky was low and gray, and mists lay on the plains, creeping softly and lazily over the marsh. The road was furrowed and muddy. The houses along the way gaped morosely; they were slovenly and sooty.

But Martin Kačur saw neither the gray sky, nor the fog, nor the sooty houses; inside he was all happiness and sunshine.

This was the period of his life when he was strong and free like never before.

He went to Bistra, to the white, one-story house; his face was at once joyous and ceremonial, as if he were standing before the church on a sun-splashed feast day. The house bore a modest, half-hidden vintner's symbol stating that wine was sold there; you would need to be thirsty to discover the clipped branches above the door. Otherwise the house bore no resemblance whatsoever to an inn. There were no trestles in front, and no drinking trough for livestock. And no tavern-keeper ever stood in the doorway, and there was never a drunk to be heard singing in the foyer. The genteel windows had been cleaned. The carters never stopped there, and on Sundays the village lads walked right past, as if it were a church. The master of the house was a well-to-do man, and he served wayfarers who didn't pay, students whom he entertained out of braggadocio, and certain refined guests who would arrive on Sunday afternoons in summer.

Kačur entered the room and took a seat at a table bedecked in gleaming white cloth. When Mrs. Sitar opened the door, he got to his feet quickly and bowed with a smile. She was a tall, attractive woman, and the only thing about her that annoyed Kačur was the quiet and slightly disdainful smile that never disappeared from her lips.

"A spot of wine? How about it, eh?"

She brought wine, ham, and bread; then she made herself comfortable at his table and folded her arms across her chest. Kačur knew that look and that smile, and yet he blushed again each time he felt her imperturbable, amused glance on his cheeks.

"So what's new with you? How are things going in Zapolje?"

"They're going all right."

"By now I'll bet you know your way around a bit. Especially with the women."

Kačur's blush deepened.

"I don't know a single woman in Zapolje."

"But they say that you're a Liberal."[1]

"I'm a what? How so?"

[1] See Note 5 in the previous chapter.

"They're saying that you can tell by somebody's face.—Have you spoken with the notary's wife?"

"Never. I barely know who she is."

Her smile was even merrier now, and a touch suspicious.

"Oh, really? Does she strike you as pretty?"

"Neither beautiful nor ugly. She's no concern of mine."

"She's in love with every young man who comes to Zapolje. Not that she's truly fond of them, but it's a habit. Her husband beats her incessantly."

"Seriously?"

Kačur's eye registered amazement.

He thought to himself, "Why is she telling me this?"

"Once, back when that young excise officer was in Zapolje," began Mrs. Sitar with a snicker, "the notary came home just at the right time—and you know what? He helped the excise officer into his coat and giggled and shook his hand. But then his wife wouldn't go out in public for a week, and when she did it was still all swollen under her eye."

The landlady let out a noisy laugh. She leaned far back in her chair and crossed her legs. Kačur's eyes met hers, which were now warmer and a bit misty.

He looked down, poured some wine into a glass, and drank it rapidly.

"What does this mean? What's going on?" he thought. Something indecent, something repulsive, something incomprehensible entered his heart.

"Well, then! There's nothing doing with the notary's wife!"

Her voice was very calm, but her eyes had again grown cool and sporting.

"And the Martinec girls? Have you had a chat with them, yet?"

"No, but they say there are a lot of them. Just today, on my way here, I saw them. There were five of them standing in the doorway."

The landlady broke into a shrill laugh.

"Five? There are ten! And God knows how many more there will be. Every one of them is worth five grand, and still nobody comes to scoop them up. They don't like the farmers and the other men are leery of their kinfolk and their piety. On Sundays they come back from vespers like geese in a row, each one of them carrying a rosary in her hand and staring down at the ground."

Kačur grew uneasy.

"God knows she is up to something. Otherwise she wouldn't be talking like this, with no rhyme or reason. What business of mine is this notary's wife? Why should I concern myself with any woman on the planet?"

The landlady noticed the ill-humor in his scarlet face, and immediately her own features became as serious and scornful as they had been before. Only the slight smile remained on her lips.

"It seems to me that you don't like stories like these. Or that you don't like women at all."

"I don't care for them, for goodness' sake!" Kačur said. He had grown almost surly.

"Would you like some more wine?"

"Yes, I'll take some more."

The proprietress picked up his carafe, avoided his eyes, and left.

"I have offended her!" thought Kačur. He was furious at himself and at her. "But what was her point? Why was she talking like that? It was not becoming to her; I've seen such women in Ljubljana, sometimes in the evening, and I would walk quickly past."

His head sank joylessly into his hands. Even his eyes were lacking their usual mirth, when the door opened and Minka entered the room. Her face was just as pale and her eyes just as black as on that morning he first caught sight of her in the bower; even her blouse had been red then as well. But at this moment he observed for the first time on her lips that same smile he had noticed on her mother: calm, nearly imperceptible, derisive, and mistrustful.

"Angry today, Mr. Kačur? In a mood?"

Kačur stood up, blushed, and squeezed her hand. She stood there placidly in front of him, smiling; she let her hand lie limply in his.

"Oh, I'm not angry or cross! I am delighted to see you, Miss Minka—as I am happy and count myself lucky even when I only get to see you in my dreams."

She sat down on the chair where her mother had been sitting a moment earlier.

"Not there, Miss Minka… Sit closer. Anywhere you wish… Not there, though!"

She looked at him in great surprise, smiled, and took a seat on the bench by the wall, right next to him.

"You seem totally different today. What has happened to you?"

He swiftly finished his drink; his face was hot and his eyes glinted with fervor.

"I'm not different! My thoughts are always intoxicated, rambling, when you are close by. And my words, they're halting and oafish like a chastened schoolboy's. All the more so today!"

Minka laughed and left her hand clasped in his.

"All the more so today! I noticed, and that's why I asked."

He didn't join in the laughter but rather met her eyes with a lingering, earnest glance. His lips tried to form words. They trembled.

"I'm going to be brazen today. I've come to you for consolation. In fact—"

His face was flushed and his eyes started to spark.

"—I could barely stand it whenever your image was absent from my thoughts. People are weak. One desires to ascend to the clouds, but it turns out one must have a cane and a prop at ground level. Look, I already told you what a magnificent calling it is when you know you're living not for yourself, but for others. And how much suffering can come with that. It's strange, and I can't understand it: there are people in that place who live only for themselves and their families. They take no heed of anyone, serve nobody; the world could go under and they wouldn't lift a finger to save it as long as their houses were still standing. They are respected individuals, and they talk a great game. But there is a handful of others, a few people of a special sort, entirely different and imprudent individuals. They do not labor for themselves, they do not live for themselves, but rather they wish to live for others in every sense of the word. They do this in spite of themselves and despite their families and the rest of the world. This is like Christ, who let himself be crucified for the benefit of others."

She was listening, but she kept her composure and the smile never left her lips. Martin Kačur noticed the beauty of her eyes, her cheeks, her lips; but he could not see her smile.

"And these people are not well liked, and their lives are hard!—The poor wretches eat their oat loaves while I bring them fine white bread: 'What am I supposed to do with this white toadstool?' they exclaim. 'Who ordered it, and who called you here?' This nation is like a sick man: it hates the doctor. But I believe, Miss, that there is no more splendid profession than that of voluntary physician, who reaps neither money nor honors but only grief and affliction."

She gazed into his face, amazed at the fire in his eyes and the color on his cheeks. She couldn't make sense of him.

Then she bent over towards him and her mien became more confidential.

"But why do it? Why do all this?"

"What's the point?" Kačur asked with surprise.

"Yes, what's the point of it? What good does it do you?"

"What good it does me? It does me absolutely no good at all! I already said that one cannot, nay, one is not allowed to derive benefit from it. Where there is profit, there is...there is no integrity. How could there be advantage when you aren't working for yourself?

When you aren't acting for yourself, you work to your own detriment!"

Her countenance suddenly grew serious.

"As I suspected: you are a poet!"

Amazement swept over Kačur again.

"Why a poet?"

"Poets don't think of their own benefit, either, and their language is as splendid as yours was just now. But at least they generate poems in the process—and you don't even produce that much!"

Kačur looked towards her and then off into the distance; the fire in his eyes had not been extinguished.

"Can't one be a poet without writing verses?" he said more calmly. "They've all been poets, all those who loved their neighbors more than themselves. And every one of their deeds is a poem."

"How oddly you're talking today, as if—as if it were the Last Supper."

This made Kačur laugh. His face brightened.

"In fact, the word was more sublime than the thing, and the gesture was greater than the word. Superfluous tragedy: a tearful 'Ode to a Deceased Beetle.' And a teacher's assistant compared himself to Christ, because he took it upon himself to found a reading circle in defiance of the mayor and the parish priest. But the Pilate-Mayor is not a whit less ridiculous than the Savior-Teacher! Still, one must bear in mind that the beetle, for whom that ode was composed, experienced no less death agony than I shall one day feel. Forgive me, therefore, my tragic speechifying; it was ludicrous, but my words were as authentic as my feelings."

Minka listened absent-mindedly to him. Her eyes held no sympathy, no enthusiasm, and no ruefulness.

"But why do you get involved in such things? Won't it bring you harm?"

"Of course it will!"

"So why do it?

Kačur, ill at ease, looked at her and pondered for a moment. He felt as if he'd been asked by a child: 'Why are you alive?'—and he didn't know how to respond.

"I don't know why! Why do I get warm all over and why does my heart skip a beat whenever I see you? I do not know the reason. Why would I let my hand be hacked off with a grin on my face, without even sighing, if you commanded? I don't know the reason! How could I order my heart to do something? It acts as it must, it goes its own way, and no thought or idea can stop it.—What would I be, then, if this great yearning in me to serve other people, to give to them the little that I have, didn't exist? Am I not lower than an animal when I recognize my true path but do not take it, because Mr. Priest is standing there at the crossroads with a cane in his hand? If I know that I need to go to the right, but I head left because there's a thicker slab of bread there? What I have is so paltry, and this life so petty and insignificant—and even this meager amount I would not offer up? It's like the miserable little donation of the widow in the Holy Scriptures: it's no less valuable than the talents donated by the rich men. And had she failed to offer it, her sin would have been counted as no less than that of the wealthy."

Minka was staring at the table; even Kačur could see that she was no longer listening. He grew furious at himself.

"What was the point of all this speechifying?—But I really didn't come here, Miss Minka, to lament or to exalt my own wretched state! It's absurd to talk this way, and my words never would've come out like this if my heart were not in such close proximity to you.—I only came here in order to see you, so that your image—which I carry in my heart—will again be vibrant and lovely. Today I just had to see you. When I leave this place, my thoughts will be much purer and my strength much greater. And tonight I'll be in need of great strength and a pure heart."

He looked at her, his eyes wide open and white-hot, his lips atremble. He wanted to say more. But he lowered his head and kissed her hand.

Minka smiled. It was that same calm, unflappable, somewhat scornful smile, and she took a long look at his disheveled hair and his youthful face, completely smooth and callow and filled with childlike trust.

"How odd you are, Mr. Kačur! I've always thought of you as a poet. Only poets talk so incoherently.—And kiss people's hands!"

She laughed while Kačur stared blankly and turned beet red. Then he smiled awkwardly, self-consciously, his eyes moistening. He was like a child with his grandma bending over him: "So why just a slice of orange? Don't you want the whole thing?"—His hands were shaking as he linked them behind her neck and kissed her on the lips.

His eyes blazed with inner fire; he looked different; his countenance was now fair and emanated a new light.

"Minka! Never—I'll never let you go!"

He was stuttering; he was intoxicated. She freed herself gently from his grasp. She was not blushing, but her eyes returned a gaze that was cheery and limpid, and her smile was as serene as before.

"Enough, Mr. Kačur!"

She abruptly burst out laughing.

"How odd your name is! Kačur, snake man, and Martin on top of that.[2] No poet should be allowed to have names like those. My mother once had a lover who was very wealthy and handsome, but ultimately she didn't care for him because he had a peculiar name. It was quite naughty."

Her laugh rang out as she looked at him with her singularly precocious but passionate eyes.

"So what was his name?" inquired Kačur, looking distracted and confused.

Minka let out a laugh, and then she pressed a handkerchief to her mouth as tears welled up in her eyes.

"You are so very like a child, Mr. Kačur! Your speech is as strange and sage as the Scriptures, and yet you are a child. God help you!"

"What did I do to her?" he thought. He did not understand her. But he heard her laughter and felt the bitterness in his heart.

[2] Additional humor comes from the fact that the name Martin resembles the Slovene word for lizard.

"Not now," he begged. "Don't laugh like that now! I've never—I've never felt like this in my life! If I were to reach out and grasp the stars—I'd never attain such bliss as this!"

He took her by the hands and regarded her with dewy eyes.

"I have so little, you see, but now I sense that it is actually a great deal, because my love is so magnificent, so infinite. Accept it as charity. My strength will climb a hundredfold, and my fortune will magnify a hundredfold, if I am consecrated by your love."

Minka smiled as she watched him, indulgence in her eyes, as if he were an adorable little child.

"Now, now, it'll be all right, Mr. Kačur. You can stop that now."

He looked at her and seemed amazed that she was just as beautiful and as worthy of all his love and desire as before.

"And not a single word more?

"A word about what?"

"There is one word that I'd still like to hear today, Miss Minka! A tender word, a friendly one—nothing else. Just one word that would remain in my heart like eternal nourishment, one word that I could think of in melancholy hours. One single word!"

"Well!"

She rested both her hands on his shoulders, like a mother, and looked into his eyes with a smile.

"But I do love you."

He kissed her hands, trembling with happiness.

"That's enough now, Mr. Kačur. You're forgetting that it's almost noon."

He didn't seem to comprehend that noontime meant he had to leave. He also would not have taken note of evening or night.

"Just one more minute! Just one brief moment!"

Loneliness was waiting for him outside. Loneliness and grief.

"Just one more!"

Minka stood up and squeezed his hand.

"You'll be coming back lots of times. Why are you so sad—as if this were the Last Supper?"

Kačur smiled, but his smile belied affliction.

"And what if we don't see each other again?"

"Why should we not see each other again?"

"If we don't see each other again the way we've been today...I have always loved you deeply, Miss Minka, and I will never forget your face."

"Why are you sad?"

"Because I love you. Where does love come from? And where sorrow?"

"There are those words again; that's how you were talking earlier!" Minka said with a smile.

"But never more!—As farewell? As we part, perhaps for a very long time?"

She shut her eyes and, with a smile spreading across her face, she offered her lips. He closed his eyes, too, and gently laid his hands on her shoulders and kissed her.

Fresh, damp air struck his face as he stepped out into the road and at first the world swayed before his eyes. He put a hand to his forehead and stopped. An annoying, incomprehensible, disagreeable sensation was already settling into his unconscious mind and heart. At the bend in the road he turned to look back; nobody was standing in front of the door and the white house seemed alien, staring back at him as mutely as if he had never crossed its threshold.

He was aware of the shadow that had descended on his heart, but he couldn't say where it had come from or why.

The day was deserted and misty like a morning. The fog was almost flashing in the drowsy, yellowish light. To Kačur the road to Zapolje seemed very long and dreary.

He encountered the peasant women and men coming from mass, the men in their manure-covered boots and the women with their skirts tucked up high. Some passed without making eye contact; others greeted him with suspicious, surly glances.

"He didn't even go to mass," remarked one peasant as he passed.

"He's marrying into the Sitar family, and he'd rather go there," answered his wife.

The man laughed.

"That's the punishment I'd wish on him!"

Kačur stopped listening; he stared blankly into space and quickened his pace.

"What have I done to them? I've never seen these people before. I've never spoken with them. And nonetheless they loathe me!"

"What is that dandy doing here?" yelled a young man standing right next to him. He put his hands on his hips so that he'd catch Kačur with an elbow. Kačur stepped to the side, and the young men moved on.

"He shouldn't be running around after the girls so much!" one of them shouted back at him.

They laughed and talked, and Kačur hurried on until he couldn't tell what they were saying anymore. He was red in the face and quaking with rage, but a smile was on his lips.

"I'll buy myself some tall boots and a nice jacket and then everything will be fine! Then nobody will ask me again whether I go to mass. It's weird to think that God would be so fixated on the piety of fops and dandies…Why did that have to be today, when I should be happy and the sun should be shining?"

When he reached his house, his room seemed very cramped and lonely and miserable. It was completely saturated with the inexplicable, undeserved, profound affliction of his heart.

"Why today?"

His thoughts returned to her, and he felt again the kiss on his lips and began to shake. The grief remained in his heart; it had nowhere to go.

"Was that love?—Was it love when she smiled and laid her hands on my shoulders…like a child?"

He had gone a long way, but he saw her face, her smile with that untroubled look in her eyes, and he recoiled from the thought.

"My heart is heavy…God knows why that is. But it makes my thoughts ugly and unjust…"

The landlady brought his lunch.

"Did you go to Bistra again, sir?"

"Yes, I did," Kačur responded gruffly.

She stood smiling at the side of the table; it was obvious that she wanted to start a conversation.

"No offence intended—but they say you go to see that woman—"

"What about that woman?" Kačur said, scowling at her.

"I'm just saying! But word is that the two of them, the mother and the daughter, make a fool out of everyone who comes into range. Quite a few have gotten burned there already and then felt the ache for some time. Now this engineer is coming and going..."

"What engineer?" Kačur was alarmed, and he turned pale.

"This dark-headed fellow...They say he will take her."

"Why are you telling me this? How does it affect me?—Take it away. I'm not hungry."

When she had closed the door, he arose and walked over to the window. The foul, narrow street lay below, and across from him was a gray building with small black windows staring unswervingly at him like a set of frigid, transfixed eyes.

"Women's babble! Obviously nothing but a woman's gossip! That is their profession and their preoccupation, and the only thing noteworthy about it is that they didn't hook her up with two or three engineers, and a few other men to boot!"

But it felt as if he had a fever in his soul, and his head ached.

"How lovely this could be! And even that miserable little bit of beauty that you manage to steal in secret gets soiled; they embitter even that one little drop of delight. And you have to do battle separately for every beautiful moment."

The gray November day waned swiftly and by early afternoon it seemed like twilight.

"Now the moment is almost upon me!" thought Kačur.

"'If you are having a rough time of it, come see me,' the physician had said. Why shouldn't I go see him? Since then I've not spoken to him at all, but I'd say his warnings are making more and more sense to me."

When Kačur went out into the street, it was gray and damp. The doctor was sitting in a room with a stove; he wore a long, multi-colored dressing gown; he had a fur cap on his head and was puffing on a long Turkish pipe. When Kačur came in, he did not stand up; he merely offered his hand instead.

"Hi, friend—so I get to see you again! Don't take it amiss if I don't get up. I am tired and I'm lazy.—Marica! Marica!"

His wife then entered the room, also wearing a long, multi-colored gown; she was tall and powerfully built, with a peremptory look in her eyes. But her lips were thick and bore a good-natured smile.

"Tea, Marica! Make it strong, and hot.—This man here is our new teacher!"

"Are you also a big drinker? Like my husband?" she asked with a laugh, standing in the doorway. Then she left.

The doctor burst out laughing as well.

"Not a bad woman.—But she must be obeyed.—Okay, so tell me now what makes you come see me! You aren't here just for the heck of it, or else you'd have come by earlier."

Kačur had intended to give a merry smile, but now he blushed.

"But you said yourself that I should drop by if something bad happened to me!"

"And now you're having a rough time of it! Hm!"

He gave him a serious look, drew deeply on his pipe, and disappeared in a dense cloud of smoke.

"So what happened?"

"It's not that anything big has occurred yet..."

Kačur was embarrassed and regretted having come.

"Well, it's not all that bad yet, and it still can be put to rights. I am after all the physician, Dr. Brinar, and there isn't an old gossip in Zapolje who knows as much as I do. First off: you intend to establish a reading circle and cultural association this evening in the Mantua. Second: you are in love with Minka, whom we saw that time we drove past; and—if you want to sing praises to my perspicacity here, I'd be much obliged—I knew immediately that you were going to fall in love with her. That's the root of all evil. The peasants are in the habit of calling on me too late; you managed to be timely enough. So, from the top again: don't found any society, in the Mantua or elsewhere; and, second, keep your distance from Bistra and its temptations, as you would avoid Satan!"

Kačur retorted angrily: "I did not come here to ask you if I should..."

But the doctor was already laughing.

"Alas, I didn't speak in the belief that you'd do what I say. Your fate is already sealed. And what a shame! In my desk drawer over there I have a full treatise, and the conclusion of that study is a piece of earnest and quite well supported advice to the government: to take all idealists, who harm humanity more than they benefit it, and lock them up in an asylum. Some lunatics run amok and kill people, which is of course not right; but the idealists represent the other extreme, and they plague humanity with their love. All they accomplish with their foolishness is to aid and abet charlatans disguising themselves as other crazy idealists to make it easier to steal gold and glory…"

"You don't really believe that!" Kačur said, smiling in hopes of seeing the physician smile too. But the doctor remained serious and now seemed to be almost sulking.

"I do think that way."

The doctor's wife brought them tea.

"It's strong enough. I'm not adding anymore rum!"

"Listen and learn," the doctor gave Kačur to understand by his doleful expression.

"So you are Minka's fiancé?" the woman asked.

"Never you mind! Never you mind!" interjected the doctor hurriedly. "Anybody can be Minka's intended…for a week."

"Don't listen to him! My husband can't say anything nice about anybody."

"As a matter of fact, nobody like that exists!" her husband confirmed.

"And Minka is an altogether virtuous girl! Likes a bit of fun—that's the way girls are."

"A bit of fun.—How true!" the doctor confirmed. He smiled. "You liked your fun, too! So, pour!"

She served their tea and took her leave.

"Maybe she was something like Minka?" Kačur thought, but then he suddenly grew livid at the idea that he had compared the broad, strapping face of the doctor's wife with Minka's creamy cheeks.

He drank his tea and his face grew hot.

"Do you know, Doctor, why I came to see you? The reason has just occurred to me: till now I had only intuited it. Don't think I'm drunk from this glass of tea. It's just that…really, my thoughts were so honorable that I could've revealed them to anyone without fear. I didn't share them with anyone, but still everybody who met me and who had any inkling of what was in my heart dragged my thoughts through the mud. I loved the girl and now I love her even more. And if she were Messalina herself[3]—who can blame me for loving her, and who can reproach me for a love that's completely pure? I wouldn't tell a friend or any honest man that his bride did not love him; if he loves her, then she is hallowed, and I can only think and repeat what he himself says about her…

Kačur fell silent; the physician had also stopped talking and was staring at the glowing stove. Kačur poured himself another cup and drank it; the tea was hot and it nearly scalded his lips.

"And all the other things you accuse me of! That I am organizing something! That's hardly worth thinking about and really has precious little significance. It will,

[3] Valeria Messalina, Roman Empress of the 1st century AD, who was the wife of Emperor Claudius and had a checkered reputation.

however, be of some slight value, and if everyone—and this shall happen!—if everyone works the way I intend to work, then our people will no longer be at the back of the pack. All of it, the whole misfortune that we've experienced, originated with one single lie: that we have no culture! And that we therefore aren't worthy to take our place among the other peoples, and we have to scrape together the leftovers while the others eat the cracklings, and fat grapes, and rich polenta!—Therefore, what is to be done? One must demonstrate that we have culture! Up to now we've just been saying that we are here; from this point on we'll have to explain what we are. It used to be work that was directed outwards, and I think it was easier; but now we're at the point where we have to work on this side of the borders. Earlier the enemies were on the outside—and the whole people opposed them. And you were a saint if you spoke up at one of the rallies. I myself, as a twelve-year old youngster, was at Sveta Trojica and heard Tavčar.[4]—I trembled and I wept. And today when I take a look at it: what kind of a nation is this for which I am prepared to give my life?—'Our nation will be as you make it—and it will know as much as you teach it.'—That's what I think. Thus it isn't my duty, but rather my life, to act in accordance with my ideas."

The doctor was puffing away ferociously; the entire room was full of smoke.

[4] Ivan Tavčar (1851–1923) was the mayor of Ljubljana for over a decade, a Liberal thinker, and a prolific and highly regarded novelist.

"Poor lad! Now, don't take this wrong! In ten, maybe twenty years it will already be different! But the point is that the clever folks always arrive on the scene too early, because if they didn't arrive too early then they wouldn't actually be so clever. To recognize the fateful hour, when it tolls, is no great trick; but to figure it out in advance—that is the art!"

He used his finger to extinguish his pipe, then drank the rest of his tea and removed his dressing gown.

"You won't find it a nuisance if I come along, will you?"

"Why would that be a nuisance?" Kačur was overjoyed.

They walked out into the night; here and there a dim lantern was burning, barely illuminating a small disk of earth next to the road. Their route was full of puddles and slime. The gleaming windows of the Mantua tavern jumped out of the darkness.

"Well then, in God's name!" laughed the doctor, as he opened the door.

"In God's name," Kačur answered, laughing in response.

The room was full of peasants and workers, and a burst of stale air hit their faces. Kačur and the doctor sat down at a small, round table under the mirror, and Kačur looked around the room. He was a bit ill at ease. He felt himself flush when he realized there were curious eyes fixed on him. He recognized immediately that, in those eyes, in those faces and conversations, there was no enthusiasm. Instead there was merely curious expectancy and, in the glances and exclamations of some of them, simply defiance and spleen. At the end of the long table an elderly farmer was seated; he was broad-shouldered and tall, smooth-shaven and happy. He was continually making eye contact with Kačur and then winking at him. At a separate table, the workers—tanners, actually—sat; Kačur fancied that he saw earnestness and good faith in evidence among them. The peasants and farm-hands were talking very loudly and slamming their glasses onto the table, causing wine to slosh out. "Nothing good lies in that quarter; they're already drunk," he thought.

The moment he stood up, ready to speak, the red-faced curate opened the door; he remained standing on the threshold and quietly looked into the room with a smile on his face. His glance disconcerted Kačur and so the first words came out in an irresolute, halting voice:

"Peasants! Workers! We have gathered together tonight to talk about a key issue..."

"Francka! Another liter!" a farmhand called out, and his table mates burst out laughing.

"So who gave him the floor? Who gave the teacher permission to speak?" queried the smiling clergyman from the door in a pleasant voice.

"That's right! Who gave the clothes-horse the floor?" shouted a drunken peasant as he slammed his empty mug onto the table.

"Nobody gave him the right!" answered the physician, also smiling and speaking in a friendly tone. "This isn't an official meeting. There's no chairman and no gendarmes. This is a place of business, and in a public house anybody who wants to can talk."

"Let him speak!" added a tanner. "We should listen to what he has to say."

The tall farmer nodded and winked at Kačur: "Just let him talk."

"I don't have a great deal to say to you, but what I want to say is important, and people of good will should take note. On an evening when I have heard all these words, some loud and some quiet, I am convinced more than ever that one thing, above all else, is necessary—"

"Belief!" the curate interrupted him in a low voice. He was still smiling.

"So it is!" a peasant cried out.

"Keep it down!" yelled the worker.

"Who's trying to boss me around?" The peasant stood up at the table and reached for his glass.

The worker said nothing; the peasant looked around the room, from face to face, and sat back down.

"Above all, one thing is necessary: studying, learning, education! I hold the view—and no one can shake it—that the cause of all our misfortune is ignorance. Stupidity, animalistic narrow-mindedness, and crudeness. That is why no nation is as unlucky as the Slovenes!"

"What did he say?" a farm-hand asked, standing up with his eyes flashing. "He should say it again so we can understand him."

"Retract that statement!" demanded the curate, taking a step into the room.

"Let him finish!" the workers shouted.

The doctor lit up a cigar and leaned towards Kačur.

"Don't even think about it—if you want to get out of here in one piece."

Kačur was stewing with disappointment, fury, and agitation.

"I won't take anything back! If you want to, then keep listening; if you don't want to, forget it! If what I say doesn't suit you, then we'll say I'm not talking to you."

"Oh, all right then. Finish!" said the curate.

"To the bitter end!" Kačur yelled out, his voice trembling. "I invited people to this tavern tonight because they are sincere in their views. I wanted to speak with them about an issue that is worth discussing.—Is it not a disgrace that these people, who learned to read at the government's behest, read nothing other than prayer books even when they aren't asleep in the pews? A disgrace, that you can't tell them anything unless you're speaking from a pulpit? A disgrace, because these people are more ignorant and uncouth than they were even in the age of peasant uprisings since they barely even read those prayer books and either sleep or puff on a cigar in front of the church during the sermon?"

"Has he come here to insult us?" a peasant shouted.

"Let's listen to him!" smiled the chaplain.

"More than anything, what we need is learning!"

"Go learn yourself," a peasant exclaimed, bursting with laughter.

"It's not your hand—it's intellect—that produces prosperity! The reason I called you all together tonight is so that we can discuss an organization, a society that will order books and newspapers and will meet to hear wise and educated people lecture on useful topics.—Such was my honorable intention—"

For the second time the doctor leaned over to him: "No wrath, no rancor!"

"Such was my honorable intention, but today we won't be talking about that. I sent out a call, but among the invitees are now others who are not worthy of that call, who should have stayed home in the stables with their livestock."

The doctor grabbed his hand firmly and pulled him down onto a stool. The tanners applauded, but the peasants and farmers rose clamorously to their feet. A glass landed on Kačur's table and wine spattered his face and coat.

"Who d'you mean, pretty boy? Who are you trying to insult, you little punk?"

The tall peasant seated at the end of the table stood up, shook his head, lurched over to Kačur's table and spread his arms in the air: "Not like this! Don't do it!"

He looked over his shoulder at Kačur and winked at him.

But the workers rose to their feet and reached for their chairs.

"Get'em!" shouted a farmhand, pulling off his jacket in a flash and hurling it to the floor.

A chair arced high under the ceiling and then landed on the table, rattling the glasses. In the middle of the room a mass of screaming men came to blows; Kačur glimpsed heated faces, foreheads swollen with veins, and clenched fists.

The owner made his way along the walls to the doctor and pressed a key into his hand.

"Through there! There!"

The doctor put his arm around Kačur, unlocked a small side door, and stepped outside with him, into the darkness of the garden.

"Here! This way!

The doctor led him along like a child; Kačur had not tasted a drop of the wine but he was swaying.

"But why was it like that? Why, doctor?"

The doctor laughed cheerfully.

"Did you think it would be any different? Of course you did! That's why I went with you.—But I knew in advance: an idealist is of no use for anything, least of all for saving his nation! This is what you get, Idealist, for your ham-handedness. Do you think they're going to remain quiet when you're labeling them nitwits? A charlatan who has honey on his tongue but orderly intentions in his mind could have told them things much worse, but he would've said it differently.—No, my dear fellow, you're not cut out for this. Noble thoughts—a lovely thing. Felicitous thoughts—a lovelier thing. So you see: a charlatan is what one needs to be!"

Kačur walked along next to him with his head down. He trembled in the cold.

"You aren't well, emotionally or physically…Come to my house; we'll drink a couple of glasses of tea, strong hot tea, and you'll forget this entire stupid affair."

He took him by the arm and led him into the room.

"Marica! Some really strong tea! Well, look at this—doesn't it hurt?"

"What has happened?" she asked.

He was pale but there were red spots on his cheeks.

"Nothing has happened," Kačur said. He had a smile on his face, but his eyes were moist.

"Okay, right away!"

She brought the tea; the doctor lit his pipe and patted Kačur on the shoulder.

"No gloomy thoughts! By no means!—What was it, after all? A banality. It could befall someone any day of the week. Disappointment! What is life besides uninterrupted disappointment? Go your merry way and say to yourself: the hell with those scumbags!"

The physician enveloped himself in tobacco smoke and said nothing for a long while. Finally he dispersed the clouds with his hand, leaned towards Kačur, and said, with an earnest look on his face:

"Do you realize that you ruined your whole life tonight? For good? Do you think that the new laws mean the teacher is no longer a servant? He is still to be a servant and a hireling—and with a heavier yoke and tighter reins than the youngest farmhand working for a big landowner. But what did you expect? The main point is this: that you were doomed from the beginning, from your birth! You can't survive with thoughts like yours; therefore neither I nor anyone else on earth can help you."

Kačur made his way to his room, laid down, and fell asleep; and he dreamt he saw Minka standing before him in that prosperous inn with her dark eyes and fair cheeks. She had her hands on her hips and was laughing in his face.

He awoke shaking and scared. Then he turned on the light and lit a cigarette.

CHAPTER THREE

Kačur was making his way to the conference room when his colleague, the teacher Ferjan, came up behind him on the stairs and grabbed his coat.

"Hang on a second!—If you don't want them to totally wring your neck in there, take my advice: be submissive, bow, and say yes, even if they offer to lynch you. These scoundrels can handle anything save pride or protest. Be humble and repentant, and smile, and by evening you'll have incited all Zapolje to rebellion, if sedition is such a big deal to you. Of me they say I am a drinker—that's the fault of my red nose—and a lousy teacher and in every respect a worthless human being. Nevertheless I'll get promoted, according to the rules of the game, because I don't get in their hair."

Kačur shook his head. He hurried the rest of the way up the stairs and knocked.

"*Herein!*"[1]

The headmaster and the priest were in the room. They were seated at a long table covered with papers and

[1] "Come in!" (German in the original.)

books. The headmaster looked at Kačur with a syrupy-melancholy mien, at once compassionate and censurious. The priest sat there looking more testy than strict.

"Bad. This is bad!" the headmaster sighed. "How could you act with such reckless abandon, Mr. Kačur?"

"To whom do I owe an explanation? And for what?" Kačur asked, his face flushing.

The priest looked up.

"You answer to me, the head teacher, and to the priest, who is the chair of the school board."

"Tell me what I've done, and I will take responsibility for it immediately!"

"That is no way to talk to the head teacher!" the priest chimed in. He gave Kačur a long, cool look to express his irritation.

"What is it, then?" seethed Kačur. He was irritated by the priest's look.

The headmaster and the priest exchanged glances. The former let out a deep sigh.

"Mr. Kačur, I'm sure you remember: I welcomed you as a colleague and as a friend. Now I see, to my enormous chagrin, that you are neither colleague nor friend. The good people of Zapolje took you in, willingly and warmly, because they were convinced that you'd be a role model and a pedagogue to their young people. They realized, I'm sorry to report, in short order that you are a bad example and a bad teacher, that you mislead the youth into committing evil acts and that you sow discord and enmity among the population…"

"What do you have to say for yourself?" added the priest.

Kačur was shaking.

"Does standing before you like this mean I am on trial? Have I already been convicted? What's the point of this sermon? Explain to me what my offences are and I will give an account of my behavior."

"What was going on last Sunday at the Mantua tavern?" inquired the priest in a frosty tone.

"You'd do better to ask the curate."

"I did ask him. And he said you were rabble-rousing against the faith!"

"He lied! I hereby testify that he is lying!"

The headmaster shook his head and looked at Kačur like he was a sinner who had already sunk very low but was still deserving of sympathy.

"Don't talk that way, Mr. Kačur! Not like that!"

"So where are we with this?" Kačur croaked. "Where are the charges against me? I want for everything to proceed in an orderly and legal fashion; I don't like sermons and I don't like warnings, either. I'm not going to stand here forever!"

"Indeed you won't," said the priest, rising slowly to his feet. "I think we are finished here," he said to the headmaster. "There's no talking with this gentleman."

He shook the headmaster's hand and departed. The other man immersed himself in papers.

"Sir!"

The head teacher looked over at Kačur as if he were just noticing him. His face was sugary and mirthful.

"Goodbye, Mr. Kačur, goodbye! I have a lot to do, a whole lot. Goodbye!"

Out in front of the school, Ferjan came up to him and laughed loudly.

"You're all red! I can see it already—they really socked it to you. How did you hold up?"

"We'll be taking leave of each other soon, my friend!" Kačur replied, forcing a smile.

"Was it that nasty? Why didn't you bow and scrape? Kiss the priest's hand?"

"Whose hand?"

"Aha! I see now what you did. What a shame! I liked you! I'm the kind of guy who only likes someone better than himself. It's true that you're a better man; but it's equally true that I am more sensible. We have to go for a farewell drink—don't deny me that."

"We'll do it."

When Kačur entered his room, he noticed a letter lying on the table. The mayor had written that he would like to speak to Kačur.

"Another sermon!" Kačur smiled. "Why not go hear this one, too? I'm already an outsider now, socially and legally. Now it's easier for me to listen, and talk and laugh about things, too…"

Right after he'd eaten, he set out for the mayor's. The door to his house was locked, so Kačur went into the shop. He watched as the mayor's thin legs carried him out of sight; as he made his getaway he was beckoning to Kačur with his finger. There were two farmers standing in the store, drinking brandy and purchasing tobacco.

The mayor then appeared behind the glass door leading to the foyer. He tapped on it softly and motioned to Kačur with his hand.

"Has he lost his marbles?" Kačur wondered. He opened the glass door and walked into the foyer. The mayor took him by the arm and led him into his private room; once again there were two glasses standing there on the table next to the bottle.

"I don't want to do it in front of people, you know? Not in front of people! They would immediately start to think—well, God only knows what they'd think. Now drink up!"

He carefully closed the door, came over to Kačur, clapped him on the shoulder, and laughed merrily. "What did you try to pull last Saturday, eh? You're a devil of a fellow! Did the priest already hear your confession? The whole shooting match? Well, did he?"

"He was waiting for me in the confessional, but I didn't show up!" Kačur smirked.

"But you didn't show up…hm."

And the mayor's face suddenly grew earnest.

"You know, the youth must be brought up in the spirit of the faith and the Kaiser, etc…You know that! One must provide an example…But you know that! Bear with me—where are you going? Huh?"

Kačur had stood up.

"Don't do it! Have I offended you? Please, just have this one drink with me.—I wanted to ask you something else…in private…"

Suddenly he broke away from Kačur, capering around the room with brisk, mincing steps and his hands behind his back. Finally he stopped and winked slyly.

"Were you serious about that…about what you said on Sunday? Tell me—I'll be truly grateful to you—do you really believe that the people, that is, that the majority of the people, will turn away from the…right reverend clergy? I would like to know your opinion on this."

Kačur, amazed, did not respond.

"I'm a Nationalist, you see?"[2] the Mayor added hurriedly. "Don't misunderstand me. There's no longer any danger of the Germanophiles[3] taking over the town. Now, ten years ago, they were in control here.—I was town councilor back at that time…"

He looked straight at Kačur, waited a moment, and then bellowed with laughter.

"So, now there are new troubles, completely new ones, and no one is at all prepared for them. Earlier it was easy: you were either Germanophile or Nationalist. And at any hour of the day you could go from being a Germanophile to being a Nationalist and be honored for making the switch. But now people have split off into such strange factions that even with your spectacles on you can't tell one from the other! They are so secret, so underground! Annoying, highly annoying!"

He clicked his tongue and gave a dismissive wave of his hand, walking rapidly around the room.

[2] See Note 5 in Chapter One.

[3] Adherents of a social and political current in Slovenia that did not emphasize national self-determination; its adherents were not necessarily ethnically German. Furthermore, many people living in Slovenia were effectively bilingual or very attached to the monarchy in Vienna, further obscuring the eventual development of their political loyalties. The word Cankar uses in this context is *nemškutar*, which has loyalist, legitimist, and anti-nationalist connotations.

"And what was it you wanted to ask me, Mr. Mayor?"

"Yes, yes, right away. So much urgency!—Well, what do you think?"

"About what?"

"How will it turn out? Will the old generation win, or the new generation?"[4]

"God knows the answer to that, but I don't!"

"You do know. You're a wily one, eh? Otherwise you wouldn't risk such a public…Is the doctor part of the new group?"

"I've never asked him."

"You don't want to reveal anything…you sly dog! So, are you of the opinion that it's still best if one inclines neither to the one side nor the other?"

"Go where your convictions lead you."

"Bah! What is that supposed to mean?" The mayor burst out laughing and then cupped Kačur's elbow in his hand. "What are you trying to say? We are alone here.—Convictions: they change constantly. But a person stays the way he or she was. Is the sun shining right this minute?"

"It's foggy out."

[4] Refers to political attitudes and groupings akin to caucuses among Slovene delegates to the Austrian parliament in Vienna. The "older" group was more conservative while the "younger" was less willing to compromise on nationalist issues. Also called "Old Slovenes" and "Young Slovenes," although, again, the differences did not lie primarily in the politicians' relative ages but rather in their political goals and methods. Similar dichotomies existed among other Habsburg nationalities, most notably the Czechs.

"See? In an hour it'll be sunny, and you will be going back on what you just said. So much for conviction!—Tell me one more thing: what exactly is the difference between the old generation and the new one? The old ones are for the faith, and the new ones are against it. Is that how it is?"

"It isn't about religion."

"So what is it about?"

"It's about progress."

"Hm! I'm for progress, too. Beautiful thing, progress...What kind of progress are we talking about?"

Kačur stared right at him without knowing what to say.

"Well, I know already. It's progress in general.—And the old grouping—what are they for?"

"They're conservatives."

"Conservatives...a beautiful thing. Hm. I'm a conservative too. Stop! What side do the Germanophiles pull for?"

"They're not on any side!"

The Mayor sprang into the air and fussed around the room.

"Not on any side! So! No side! Sensible folks...Ah, those were grand times!"

He dashed through the room, his hands behind his back and his head bowed; suddenly he stopped in front of Kačur.

"Aha! So you're still here!"

He gave him a grave look and shook his head.

"It was not good, sir; it was not right, what you did last Sunday! It wasn't appropriate. It truly wasn't!"

Kačur stood up and reached for his hat.

"Now, what can I criticize you for? You are young and aren't yet intimately familiar with the duties of…the priestly estate…etc…You know! Well then, goodbye!…Through the store, please, through the store. The people don't necessarily need to…All right, goodbye!"

Kačur walked out to the street through the shop as the mayor disappeared into the darkened entrance hall.

"Scoundrel!" he thought to himself, hurrying away in the slimy street. "Such a…He's not even up to the level of scoundrel!"

Evening was falling already as he walked towards Bistra.

Fog hung over the landscape, but a full moon shone through it from its spot high above the hill.

Then he halted in the middle of the road.

"What am I supposed to be doing there? Isn't everything they've told me true? Didn't I suspect it myself, the first minute I was here? If everything else has failed, collapsed ignominiously, what do I need there?"

And, still absorbed in the sad prospect that he would return and be forgotten, he actually quickened his step and hurried along. His heart was beating stronger.

"The beginning miscarried, that's all. Why shouldn't I keep venturing forward, even if I stumbled on the first step? I was too clumsy—that's the whole trouble.—I'll explain to her how it happened, and the telling of it will suddenly make it funny, and I'll laugh and Minka will laugh, too. Verily, the world has never seen a Redeemer this odd! And never such pitiful deliverance.—But nonetheless, it seems to me the whole farce was not in vain; the people will have something from it. If nothing else, they are still hot-headed, and hot-headedness is always useful. Maybe they still have some fight in them, and then major antagonism will develop, and antagonisms are always fruitful. It was not squandered! And it is true that one is lavishly rewarded for even the smallest thing we do that is to our own detriment but for the well-being of our neighbor!"

His thoughts grew more cheerful, and his overheated face along with them.

"So where is the detriment to me?" he thought with a smile. "They're going to transfer me. That's the limit of the unpleasantry. I've gotten to know the Zapoljans, and thoroughly. So tomorrow I get to know the people of Zagorec, perhaps, and the day after tomorrow those in Zaplanec. In this manner I will roam through every part of this beautiful homeland, with bundle and pilgrim's staff, and there'll be no patriot anywhere with a more detailed knowledge of the people than I have. There've been times when I sorely wished for the chance to travel across this land of mine, through all its nooks and crannies.—And now I will do it, and on the government's nickel! And I have neither wife nor child: a free man!"

At that same instant a shadow flickered across his face.

He had never before thought of Minka as other than a girl in a red blouse, with a pale face and black eyes, the pretty daughter of a wealthy tavern-owner—with whom he would sit alone in a room, and whose small round hands he would kiss, and to whom he would utter sweet nothings. It had never occurred to him that things might be different someday, and that he might have to stand there in front of fat old Mr. Sitar, wearing a black suit, red in the face, bashful and trembling.

He waved his hands in order to scare away that odious thought.

"Stupidity! She is still a child! Me, too—how am I any different? This is…a vile thought. The devil sent it my way so as to lead me astray…"

In the door stood the woman of the house.

"Minka is in the park!" she said to him as she smiled in greeting.

"She's in the park now? In the dark? With this fog?"

"That's what she told me. Maybe she's not in the park. Go check it out!—And what have you been up to recently in Zapolje?"

"Nothing much, ma'am!"

"Nothing?" she chuckled. "Everyone says they're going to run you out of there. That you are mixed up in some awful stuff."

"Oh, that! Well, these people got into a brawl in the pub, and I, the one who wasn't fighting, will get the punishment for it. Nothing else happened!"

Mrs. Sitar wagged an accusatory finger at him.

"They're talking about some completely different things, too! I never would have thought you could be like that, the way you show off that innocent face of yours."

"So, what did I do?"

She laughed out loud.

"The way you ask is so charming! Like a little virgin maiden.—Oh, go find Minka! And then you'll come by for a drink, no? You must be thirsty."

She laughed even more loudly; Kačur recoiled from that laugh because he did not understand it.

"I'll come."

The park was peaceful, deserted; the mist dropped lower and lower over the leafless, black, dank trees; the sand was mingled with mud and it readily gave way beneath one's feet.

"How am I supposed to find her here?" Kačur thought, walking this way and that across the sandy paths. Close to the gazebo, along the fence, he glimpsed a shadow and a pale face.

She moved rapidly towards him, stopped three steps away, looked him right in the face, and broke out in laughter.

"Martin Kačur!"

"That's me" Kačur responded. The blood shot to his face and he started to tremble.

"How did you find your way here?"

"The lady of the house informed me that you were in the park."

"Why didn't you stay with my mother, in the warm house? It's dark and cold out here."

And indeed Kačur was shaking all over with cold. He looked at her and found her much changed. Her face was impassive and her glance was distant and contemptuous.

He turned around slowly; his head was swimming.

"Goodbye."

"Where are you off to? Why'd you come here? I'm not chasing you away! Do stay a while!"

She approached and took his hand.

"How odd you are! Like a child! Well?"

She pressed her body to his and offered him her lips. He enveloped her stiffly with his arms, hugged her hard, and kissed her on the lips and cheeks. His head was buzzing and his breathing grew labored.

Slowly she emerged from their clinch.

"So hot-blooded!—I like you, because you are so wickedly foolish!"

Kačur stood there, eyes fixed upon her, saying naught. Minka laughed.

"Honestly! It's true! Because you are terribly foolish! Anything you say—it makes me laugh so hard I cry when I think back on it."

"Don't laugh! Don't joke with me!" Kačur entreated. "Seeing you laugh brings no joy to my heart. Tonight, Minka, tonight you should refrain from being funny! I'm seeing you for the final time.—I feel this in my bones, just as if God had revealed it to me!"

"How am I supposed to refrain from laughing when what you say is so weird? But if you don't want me to, I won't laugh. All right?"

She knitted her brow, set her lips firmly, tightened her cheeks so much that wrinkles appeared—and then roared with laughter.

"Who can stay serious in your presence?"

He took her hand, smiling himself now, but his smile was wan.

"I love you more than I ought to. My love is too great, and that's why it's ridiculous. But go ahead and laugh! Your face is wondrously beautiful when you're happy, and nothing makes your eyes sparkle more..."

She immediately got a serious look on her face.

"Why do you speak with such wisdom, so slowly and solemnly, like a ghost at midnight? It's not charming. In the worst case it's absurd. When you do it one time, it's nice. Nice like a poem that someone reads through once. But to do it all the time: woooo, woooo, woooo! What is up with that? People embrace, they kiss, they laugh.—Basta!"

"Don't be angry with me! I told you that I love you too much. Forget about the 'too much' part and just think about that 'I love you.'"

He was trembling, his eyes moist and imploring.

Minka seemed distracted; her eyes showed neither merriment nor irritation.

"When are you planning on leaving?"

"Leaving what?"

"Well, Zapolje. I take it you are going away. So they say."

"I don't know yet. Soon!"

"Well, now! Wherever you end up going...don't think ill of me!—And maybe you'll come see us sometime?"

She offered her hand.

"Is this farewell, then, Minka?" exclaimed Kačur.

"What else is left?" she wondered aloud, and then started laughing.

She propped her hands on her hips, angled her head, and pursed her lips.

"Well?"

He kissed her. Trembling, he remained standing in front of her.

"And—is there nothing more, Minka?"

"What else should there be? How annoying you are! One more time, then!"

"Nothing else at all!"

He looked at her with his dark, timid eyes and slowly turned away.

"Goodbye, Minka!"

"Goodbye!"

"Impossible! It can't be like this," he thought. Then he stopped and looked back.

She had lifted the hem of her skirt and was walking along the mucky path back towards the gazebo.

"Hey there, Miss Minka!" he called out. "I take it you're expecting somebody?"

"You bet!" she answered, roaring with laughter and waving at him. Her pale face gleamed out of the darkness, illuminated by an unseen source of light.

Kačur staggered, wailed, and beat a hasty retreat from the park. Hold the thoughts! Hold the emotions! To the muddy path! To the wide road! He hurried along, hunched over, with sweat rolling off his face.

"There—what village is that over there?"

He reached Zapolje. The taverns were still lit up. They had customers in them, sitting in warm rooms, in the bright light. They were laughing and chatting and were unfamiliar with melancholy.

He opened a door. In the nicer dining room there were only three guests sitting around a table all decked in white: a teacher, who was a young, full-figured woman with lively, shrewd eyes and a whale of a double chin; a drowsy, awkward young revenue officer in bad need of a shave; and Master Ferjan.

"Look what the cat dragged in!" Ferjan said, as he leapt out from behind the table. His face glowed red, and his eyes spat fire. "Wow, the way you look! Are you sick? You're all pale! You're all grimy! Where are you coming from?"

He shook his hand and then pulled him over to the table.

"Where was I going?"

Ferjan guffawed.

"He's drunk, folks, drunk! Where were you going? You've arrived in the Mantua! The site of your glory and renown! So now, have a seat, Mr. Idealist!—What? Where to then?"

Kačur stripped off his coat and took a seat at the table.

"Nothing doing! You're going to have a drink with me! You promised you'd go drinking with me before you departed.—Hey, sleepy-head taxman! This is Kačur. You two haven't met yet. But, then again, it doesn't matter if you get to know each other or not. Sleep on!"

"I've stayed because you requested it of me, Ferjan. I'd actually rather be spending tonight at home."

Kačur stared at the table and put his head in his hands.

The other teacher spoke up: "This really is a big deal. They don't need to persecute somebody on the basis of such a triviality! This does not sit well with me, either."

"That's all fine and dandy, Miss Matilda, and it's to your credit," Ferjan announced solemnly. "But acts of solidarity don't count in a pub!—I know you well, Kačur!

This farce doesn't really have you worked up.—What's eating you?"

Kačur fixed his calm, thoughtful gaze on him but gave no answer.

"All right, then. Let's drop it. We don't need to worry about what's lurking in the closet. Every person has his or her sacristy; that's nobody else's business. I have a place like that, too!"

The woman teacher was smiling at Kačur.

"Rumor has it that you were in love with Minka, the girl from Zapolje."

"I was!"

"Are you still in love with her?"

"I am!"

"Spoken like a true man!" Ferjan interjected. He banged his fist on the table.

"She's with that engineer now, right?" the teacher inquired.

"I don't know!" Kačur replied, his mouth quivering. "If they love each other, that's just great. I love her just as before!"

Ferjan drained a full glass at one go and then showed his temper: "Hey, Matilda, you hag! If you don't lay off him immediately, I'm going to throw you out onto the street! What do you care about whom he likes or doesn't like? Does he turn your head, too? Huh? Are you checking him out? He hasn't even noticed you. He's too smart for that."

The young revenue officer roused himself and reached across the table to shake Kačur's hand.

"Yep, he's a smart one. Smart."

This behavior enraged Ferjan immediately.

"Why don't you be quiet, since no one is asking you anything? Go to sleep!"

The man fell asleep again.

"Francka!" Ferjan called out. "Lock the door, so that every Tom, Dick and Harry can't listen in on what these good folks are up to."

"I'm leaving, Ferjan!" Kačur said and stood up.

All at once Ferjan's expression changed completely. His face was credulous and almost timid. He grabbed Kačur's arm and made him sit down next to him.

"Man, oh, man. Do you think you're the only one? Why can't you believe that even I was once in the same position you're in tonight, and like you were last Sunday evening? You know, I'm mostly just an alcoholic. My nose didn't lie to you—I did. But believe me: you wouldn't have been able to talk as you did on Sunday if it weren't for me. You intend to save all the world at once, the whole nine yards—and I drink and just give out homeopathic powders from time to time, first to this person and then to that—and they take it and don't even know what they've gotten. Well, that's not my method. No! Why a method? It's my nature! I don't want anybody to disrupt my drinking! and I do not want to change pothouses, either. One day something in Dolenjsko, then one in Vipava, finally a Styrian.—Nope! I'm not cut out for that."

"But what is the point of all this?" Kačur asked, dumbfounded.

"Indeed! It's unnecessary."

Ferjan leaned over even further and put his head on Kačur's shoulder.

"I had planned to tell you something altogether different, but I got rather carried away.—Say, would you like some money?"

"What?"

"I mean, I'm just going to drink it up anyway!—See, I'm intoxicated!"

He turned his befuddled gaze to the woman.

"What's with you?"

"Drunkard!"

"God'll punish you yet. He'll make you my wife!"

Kačur had leaned back in his chair and covered his eyes with the palms of his hands.

"How ugly, how hideous this all is!"

"What's hideous?" marveled Ferjan.

Kačur stood up and quickly donned his coat.

"No offence intended, Ferjan! I'm ill—you can see that.—Good night!"

And he quickly lurched away. He reached his house and lay down on the bed but didn't blow out the light. His eyes flashed feverishly.

The fact that he'd been sitting in a tavern, drinking and talking, completely fled his mind.—Instead he saw before him a pale face, laughing, and it seemed to him that he had just come from there, just this minute, and he could perhaps even return.

"But all is lost! Once and for all!"

He thought back over his ludicrous actions and laughed out loud.

"Who needs it? What good is it? I am just a wretch with nowhere to put his head, with nobody to call his own on the planet. And I want to give of my poverty to others? Not a speck of love has been mine to savor, and I'm supposed to fill up bushels of it for others? 'Oh, help yourself'—that's what they said to Christ. O, God!"

Thereupon he fell asleep. His breath rattled in his throat, and he cried out in his dreams.

PART II

CHAPTER ONE

Fortunately for Martin Kačur, and to the benefit of the moral state and sense of unity of the Slovene nation, Blatni Dol's teacher of many years died in February, and Kačur moved there bag and baggage.

The village was long and spread out, but it was dark and dirty to a degree that Kačur had never before witnessed. In the streets of Blatni Dol, the mud[1] overflowed into broad lakes, even when the sun was already shining on the rest of the world. The village lay in a deep depression, guarded on all sides by hills overgrown with low scrub that was as dark and desolate as the village itself.

"Who had the bright idea of settling in this wasteland?" Kačur wondered. "It could only have been smugglers, army deserters, poachers, and outlaws!"

As he strode along the village street, he saw someone piling manure behind the church. It was a thickset old man with a broad, sunburnt face, bushy gray brows, and

[1] A pun on the repetition of the word mud, *blato*, which also figures in the name of the town itself, "Muddy Valley" or "Muddyvale."

an unshaven face resembling a field of gray stubble. He wore a dirty linen shirt and a vest of coarse cloth; he had rolled his trousers up to his knees and wrapped his legs in burlap. Kačur was astonished to see a clerical collar under the old man's chin.

"Who are you?" said the old man, turning to face him.

"I am the teacher. I arrived yesterday evening."

"And I am the priest."

He kept on shoveling and paid no more attention to Kačur. A bewildered Kačur walked away.

"Tomorrow is Sunday, right?" the priest called after him.

"Yes, it is!"

"Come see me at noon!"

Kačur moved his things into the school, which was a grim peasant cottage with a thatched roof, hard by the church. In the foyer, in his room, and in the classroom it stunk like a stable. When he walked into the entrance hall of the house, he caught sight of a lean, tall woman, with her skirt hiked up high and a birch rod in her hand, chasing after a shabbily dressed urchin. Both disappeared in an instant through the doors to the stable, and then Kačur heard yelling and cursing in the distance.

He took a look at the classroom: dreadful! It was a long, low room, in the middle of which stood a few worm-eaten benches, with lots of carvings and ink spatters. Up front was a crudely built table with one short and three long legs, and behind it was a chair, of a sort once fashionable but now spitting up its stuffing. The walls were black and damp; above the table hung a picture of the Kaiser, but the stove emitted so much smoke in winter that its surface had blackened and was caked in soot; below it had been written in great letters:

THIS IS A PICTURE OF FRANZ JOSEF I.

He went into his room, but his distress did not diminish. It was exactly as murky and bleak as the classroom, with the only differences being that its long, narrow shape seemed to indicate its former service as a nook for the elderly and that it had a bed in it.

Shouting could once again be heard out in the foyer, and the woman with the birch rod returned. She went past him, directly into his room, and then from his room on into the classroom.

"Hey, auntie—who are you? Are you the housekeeper?"

She did not turn around or answer.

"Hey, can't you hear me?" Kačur cried.

The ragamuffin reappeared in the entrance and laughed out loud.

"Why are you yelling at her like that when she cannot hear? She's deaf, you know...She only hears when you yell into her ear!"

"And who are you?" Kačur asked the dubious-looking boy.

The little fellow looked him up and down warily. Then he thumbed his nose at Kačur and made his getaway out into the streets.

"These people are smugglers and bandits and nothing but!" Kačur thought to himself. He went over to the woman and yelled into her ear as loud as he could:

"I am the teacher! The teacher! Do you understand?"

The woman dropped her broom, raised both hands to her face, and shouted back at him, louder still:

"Jesus and Mary, did you ever scare me!"

"Are you the housekeeper?"

"What?"

"I asked whether you are the housekeeper!"

"I'm sweeping!"

"Go to hell!" Kačur yelled and then turned around and left.

"For God's sake," he thought. "Is there not one Christian soul in this den of iniquity? I am not surprised, unlucky chap, that you prepared such a wretched death for yourself!"

He set out for the tavern, the finest building in the village. It was almost taller than the church, even counting the steeple, and it sported a better coat of whitewash than the rectory.

The tavern-keeper also served as mayor, a stout, jovial man with a puffy face. He had such a small forehead that his hair hung down all the way over his eyebrows.

"Could I take my lunches and suppers here? For a monthly fee?"

"You're our teacher, no?"

"Yes."

"Of course you can have your lunches and suppers here. The other teacher used to come here, too; but now he's dead, and it was an unchristian death he met with."

"How was it unchristian?"

"Well, he crept around like a shadow but never exchanged a word with anyone. He didn't utter a word in the school, either, and he just kept beating the children till they all went and jumped out the window. Then he locked himself in his room and didn't come out for an entire week. And it was on the eighth day that he hanged himself."

"No wonder!" Kačur remarked lugubriously.

"What do you mean, no wonder? Things weren't going badly for him! He had enough to eat and drink. What more does a person need?"

Kačur made no reply.

"One would have to be very stalwart to live here," he thought. "And very rich in intellectual life and tremendously dignified. And I am not particularly robust, I have no particularly rich intellectual life, and I am shackled to this world; I have not lifted myself above it."

"There won't be a lot of work for you," the mayor continued. "At times the school is completely empty, especially in summer. That's when you can lie down in the shade and take a nap instead of duking it out pointlessly with the little brats. There'll be more of them in the winter, but mostly children of the tenant farmers, who have nothing with which to heat their homes. They come to school to get warm…But what do these snot-nosed kids need to learn? Let them go to work! I know how to read also.—And how does it profit me? I can read German; I learned it from the soldiers. But our books aren't written in German and I can't read the German ones anyway, because they are written in a language that the Devil himself couldn't make heads or tails of. In the barracks we talked differently!"

"But what happens when a letter comes from the authorities?" inquired Kačur.

Without a word the mayor raised his hand and pointed his finger over his shoulder. Kačur looked around and saw in the unlit corner a gangly, tall man seated there, looking neither particularly young nor old, with his eyes on the mayor and him and an infinitely insolent and cunning expression on his face. His pointed chin was covered with long red hairs; his watery eyes blinked and seemed to laugh. Rather poorly dressed, he was wearing a threadbare old suit with coat-tails and tight-fitting pants that were too short.

"He knows German," whispered the mayor, nodding. Then he slowly turned around in the squeaking chair.

"Come over here for a minute, Grajžar!"

The secretary swiftly finished his drink, walked over to the table, and bowed.

"Good day, sir!"

By the fast, smooth way he pronounced words, Kačur could tell the man was from Ljubljana.

"This is our teacher!" the mayor explained. "And this is my secretary!"

The secretary sat down with them at once. Kačur studied his face but couldn't tell whether he was twenty years old or forty.

"I think we're going to hit it off just fine. I, for one, am the intelligentsia in this blessed locale." The secretary spoke rapidly, winking at Kačur and nodding his head slightly towards the mayor.

"What did you say?" asked the mayor. "Was it something positive or something negative?"

"I stated that I am the intelligentsia in this place!"

"What is that?"

"Intelligentsia is the Slovene term for municipal secretary, because it starts with him and ends with the attorney."

"What peculiar words this guy digs up!" laughed the mayor. "Every few minutes a new one occurs to him. He recently hornswoggled the higher-ups for three whole months by corresponding with them only in Italian; he claimed we had a municipal secretary who only spoke Italian. Ultimately I threw him in the clink till he got used to the idea of writing in German again."

"Why do you correspond in German? From Blatni Dol of all places?" Kačur wanted to know.

"How else, when this cad here pretends he can't write Slovene any more? Last year he was still able to do it, but now he says he's had a stroke in that part of his brain where the Slovene alphabet is located."

"Is that true?" Kačur marveled. He gazed at the secretary, whose face was so melancholy and distorted that it made Kačur even more perplexed.

"What is wrong with you?"

"Nothing! The stroke!"

The mayor roared with laughter.

"You see? That's how he always is! When he's feeling lazy, he lies down and sleeps and does nothing but eat and drink for a week, saying that he's had a stroke. Right about now he'll be wanting something to drink.—Mica!"

The girl placed a liter of wine on the table and the secretary's face brightened at once.

Dusk was falling. Kačur drained his glass and got to his feet.

"Leaving already?" asked the mayor. "Well, now, you'll be coming back on a daily basis. We'll come to terms later about that payment."

The secretary came out onto the street right behind Kačur.

"Sir, do you really think I'm that much of an idiot?"

"I do not!"

"I'll tell you this: if you don't create your own diversions here, you might just croak. Would you believe that I occasionally stand in front of the mirror and tell myself jokes?—Good night!"

And with that he trotted back inside.

"So that's what one must do!" Kačur thought.

He was freezing cold when he got back to his room. The black walls glared at him with a weird, dead feeling. Kačur felt like he'd been locked away in prison; his chest tightened with fear and his courage drained away.

When he had put out the light and lain down, he saw quite clearly before his eyes the face of his fellow teacher who had prepared his own unchristian end. He was pale and had a long, pointed beard, and he had eyes that sat far back in their sockets.

"Once I was in the state you're in tonight! And you, too, will someday be in the condition I was in when I locked myself away! My thoughts used to soar up to the clouds, as joyous and bright as the sun; but then they perished in this muck. Do not entertain the hope that you will even gain a foothold, that you will realize a shadow or a nostalgic token of your ideas. Soon you will feel the vampire astride your chest, clinging to your back, drinking, slurping out of your bitter veins and straight out of your heart. Your limp, bloodless hands will hang at your sides and you won't be able to defend yourself! That's how life will empty you. That's how the vampire will drain even the last drop from you, until you lock yourself away as I did."

"Let me go!" a frightened Kačur screamed, as he sprang from his bed.

He bolted the door and then felt his way along the wall until he reached his bed again; his entire body dripped with sweat.

He dozed into the morning hours, peevish and lost in thought. The bells were ringing for mass, and he headed for the church, since there was nowhere else to go. The inside of the church building was even more squalid and desolate than the outside. The pictures on the walls and ceiling had turned black and blurred into what looked like large damp spots. The altars stood crooked, with wooden saints that tilted and wobbled whenever someone passed by. The pulpit, also of wood, resembled a big empty straw basket resting on a stumpy pillar.

The church was already full; the space clear up to the altar was full of standing women. The air was humid and stale. People coughed and spat, as women's skirts rustled and by the entrance two farmhands argued and finally began throwing punches at each other. Some little urchin stood laughing beneath the pulpit until an old farmer grabbed him by the ears and hounded him out of the building.

Kačur stood observing the people from a spot in front of the sacristy. It seemed to him that the hostile shadows of Blatni Dol rested on their faces, shadows of desolate roads full of puddles, of gray houses, and even of his dark and cheerless quarters. Among the women standing in front of the altar he saw a voluptuous girl with a kerchief of red silk on her head. She wore a light red blouse and a green skirt. Her face teemed with vitality, and you could scarcely find the shadow of Blatni Dol on those full and somewhat sultry lips, or in her steady, expressionless brown eyes. Kačur kept looking at her and was not even aware that he was staring at her uninterruptedly until the sexton rang the bell and the priest came out to the altar.

The mass struck him as curious, too, and yet he knew that it could not be otherwise in Blatni Dol. In this church building, on this altar, the smell of incense was different from other places, and the candles lacked their usual festive gleam. It was all so run-of-the-mill, bleak, earth-bound. The priest trod heavily, firmly, out to the altar—like a man in the field behind his plow—and swung the tabernacle open with a calloused hand as if it were the door to a barn. After the offertory he went into the sacristy, removed the chasuble, and climbed up to the pulpit. When he had pronounced the blessing and finished the prayer, he blew his nose into a broad, green cloth, and Kačur watched, awestruck, as everyone else, both men and women, produced handkerchiefs at the same time. An old farmer standing behind the door blew his nose into his hand and then spat on the floor. Then the priest started his homily.

"Christian men and women! A new teacher has come to Blatni Dol. A young man. There he stands, in front of the sacristy!"

Everybody turned to look at him.

"Deal honorably with him. Otherwise you'll have to answer to me!—What does that little urchin there have to laugh about? Hey, you, standing next to him—grab him by the hair and give him a good tug.—Don't treat this teacher the way you did the last one, whom you renegades drove straight to hell. Woe to anyone who lays a hand on him or even looks at him askance. I'll jerk such a knot in that person's tail that he'll remember it for the rest of his life! And for absolution after that he can go to Father Nace in Razor, or Father Brlinček in Močilnik—because he won't get it from me. And send your children to the school as often as you can. When there's no work for them in the field, don't let them just hang around, poking around in nests and burrows or playing ball. Don't let a jackanapes like that cross my path! I'll give him a wicked thrashing and send the gendarmes to visit his father. Do you really think we're paying the teacher to do nothing? He'd be stealing our money if he were just to stand there with his cane in the school with nobody else around! In that case I'll quit saying mass and taking confessions and administering Holy Communion. I'll just pocket your money. And it'll be gulp-gulp-gulp and zzz-zzz-zzz all the live-long day. Let our teacher be told that he should bring our guttersnipes over to the church, as is right and proper. And he should only thrash them, really knock them about, when it's necessary. And it's always necessary! They're not going to learn anything anyway, because they are too stupid, so let them at least learn to be afraid of the cane.—Otherwise, what still needs to be said here is this: do not steal, do not brawl in the taverns, and let the grandpas leave the grannies in peace, and the grannies the grandpas, or else watch out! Amen!"

During the sermon, which left Kačur utterly shocked, and the second part of the mass, he looked over only infrequently at the girl in the red kerchief. But she remained in his sight like a bright image that sticks with you after you shut your eyelids. And he saw her again as he left the church and headed towards the presbytery. The most remarkable thing, he thought, is that nothing about her reminds me of Minka except for the red blouse. The new woman's face was not white—the whiteness of a white-hot iron—and her eyes were not black and radiant, and no smile was to be found upon her lips. Nonetheless his heart gravitated towards her, quivering and involuntarily, and his blood was hot, even while his thoughts remained cold.

The priest greeted him cheerily. He sat at his table, in his shirt-sleeves and without his collar. He poured Kačur and himself a drink of schnapps.

"I've never heard a homily such as that one," Kačur noted with a smile.

"What, wasn't it a good one?" the priest rebutted him. He had a serious look on his face. "What would you preach to those morons and highwaymen?"

Kačur realized that the priest was right, and he didn't answer. They ate a quick lunch. A corpulent, pimply woman eyed Kačur crossly as she put the food on the table. The priest took aim at her with his thumb.

"It's harder to get rid of a woman like that than it is a legitimate wife! Do you think it would help if I chased her off? She'd scold and nag me so much I'd barely be able to set foot outside the presbytery.—This food is burnt again!"

"Lord knows who the nut job[2] is around here!" the woman rejoined. She eyeballed them contemptuously and slammed the door.

"Do you know what's irritating her? That I failed to invite you here yesterday, and that I don't want her to join us at the table. She likes the young fellows."

He clasped his hands over his stomach and laughed like a horse.

"Well, what can you do?—Do you intend to remain long in Blatni Dol?"

"I've made no plans. I didn't want to come here and I don't believe it would help if I wanted to leave. I'm just thinking one thing: I won't remain here for very long. Because otherwise I'll perish, perhaps in as sad a state as my predecessor and colleague."

"You have to get accustomed to things; that's all! I acclimated, too. And now I no longer want to leave here, and if I did want to go away, I couldn't—the people

[2] A joke built on the similarities in sound of the Slovene words *prismojen*, barmy, and *zasmojen*, singed, which the priest used in the previous sentence.

would block my path with scythes!—And where am I supposed to go? I've been living here for twenty years and have gone native. Like a peasant.—How could I have survived otherwise? There is no alternative life: either be with the people, be like them, or die! And now there's nowhere else I wish to go. Anyway, where could I? People would ridicule me everywhere, and I would be as awkward as a bat on a sunny day."

"Were you also assigned here as punishment?"

"You betcha! Who would take it upon himself to move to Blatni Dol? But the reason for my punishment—I don't even know it anymore. When a person is used to jail, he forgets the sin. You, too, young man, will be shoveling shit one day!"

"Is there no other way out? I mean, there are one's thoughts and ideas. And at least one does have books!"

"Wrong! Take a look at my library. The breviary is in there and nothing else. I used to have a number of books, but she probably used them as kindling. And I don't hold it against her. Thoughts, books—they just make people dissatisfied. They make you weak. Sick. But if you work in the field, and handle livestock, then you won't plague yourself with ideas and you'll live to a ripe old age. I'm already seventy years old, and I could still pin you as if you were a toddler. And I'll live to see a hundred!"

"But what's the point?"

"Aha! See? That's where your thinking gets you! It makes you grumpy and embittered! What's the point of living? Every year I have my special worries: how will the grain turn out, whether the livestock is flourishing, and what the vintage is going to be like. I turn around and spring and fall and winter have passed. But you pore over your books and moan: what's the point of living?—I have heard of people who put an end to their own lives, and they are mostly people who concern themselves with books. But there's never been a farmer who strung himself up; I've never heard of an ear of wheat doing away with itself."

Kačur was depressed. His heart felt leaden, dead.

"So what distinguishes a human being from an animal?"

"Faith!"

Kačur hung his head.

"But these twenty years here, sir, they aren't all there is to life! There was, previously, another life…before the Fall. I tasted it, too!"

The priest looked away. He was staring into the distance from under half-closed lids.

"There was that!—But what's the use of it now? What am I supposed to do with that?"

He smiled. His face brightened and took on an oddly tender expression.

"Was I ever an 'agitator' back then! That was long ago. I was a Nationalist too early. Nowadays any old curate can be a Nationalist without risk to himself, but early on it wasn't that way. Well, I was still young, and stupid. When you're young, you believe that the whole world revolves around you! You have tremendous obligations, and a mighty calling, and a solemn mission, and if you don't carry it out, then woe to the peoples of the earth! But the only reality to it all is that you have too much blood in your veins. That was certainly the case with me. And what do you think my grand and solemn mission was? I taught boys to sing. Namely those patriotic songs that a person sings when he or she is inebriated. And I raved about the poet Koseski,[3] and about Toman,[4] too! Is Toman still alive?"

"He has since died."

"May he rest in peace…And what is your calling? Your mission?"

Kačur blushed. He did not know how to respond.

"Hm, what could it be—the same thing it always is? You want to work with the people, right?"

The priest was looking out the window when he leapt out from behind the table.

"Oh, you damned guttersnipe! You don't even spare my garden in the winter! At least wait, you little monster, until the pears are ripe! I know who you are. You're one of Mrkin's kids!"

He retreated from the window, still flushed and exasperated.

"Out of sheer malice he goes and cuts off the grafted branches with his pocket knife. Don't waste your time on these people! They know themselves what they need: they eat, they drink and they die. What else could they want? The only folks who work with the people are the

[3] Janez Vesel Koseski (1798–1884), Slovene Romantic poet, lawyer, and patriot linked to the Old Slovene political current.

[4] Lovro Toman (1827–1870), Slovene poet who made wide use of folk motifs and, like Koseski, is generally considered a minor figure by literary historians.

ones who betray them. They are themselves different, alien, and they hold that the people need to be different, too!—You see, I settled amidst these people and have been living among them for twenty years and then some. I do not believe in the least that they want to find a way out of this dung-heap into some higher realm. Let things stay as they are. The locust belongs in the field, the horsefly on the horse, and the midge in the tavern!"

With that, the priest stood up and Kačur started to take his leave.

"Come visit me once in a while, but not too often, for I have a great deal to do! And don't fret or trouble yourself too much about the school. You aren't going to accomplish anything anyhow.—Goodbye!"

Kačur left without knowing where he should go next. He shuddered to think of his room; the streets were deserted and bleak; the naked black mountains towered over the canyon. There was nowhere for the eyes to range, and no place for the heart to roam either. At one end of the village, at the bottom of the hill, stood a long, low building that was very dirty and uninviting. A publican's wreath hung above the door. No noise escaped from the barroom, and the windows were so grimy that no one could see through them in either direction.

In the entrance hall stood an elderly, corpulent woman who was washing glasses.

"Is this really a tavern?" he asked.

"You bet it is!"

He started to enter but then stopped in his tracks; his fear exceeded his exhilaration. She was sitting by herself at a table, wearing the red blouse and the green skirt.

She looked around at him and slowly rose to her feet.

"What would you like, sir?"

"Some wine!"

She walked past him, swaying her hips, her full lips gathered into a smile.

"I will never come here again!" The thought passed through Kačur's head in the midst of his unfathomable anxiety. He reached out his hand for his hat but then sat back down and waited.

She brought his wine. After setting the bottle in front of him, she looked him in the eyes with a smile. Then she sat down with him and propped her arms on the table. Kačur saw the dimples in her powerful, rough hands and the tightly stretched blouse over her thick forearms and full breasts.

"You haven't been here long, mister. I saw you in church today for the first time. You're going to get bored in Blatni Dol."

"Bored, huh? Yesterday evening I was already bored! That's why I'll be coming here pretty frequently..."

Hardly were those words out of his mouth when he was ashamed of them. She chuckled, showing the dimples in her cheeks, now, and her bright white teeth.

"Why shouldn't I talk to her?" Kačur thought to himself. "Why can't I horse around with her a bit?"

And that first shadow from Blatni Dol—still light, barely visible—descended over his heart, and he himself sensed, with trepidation that was still only half-conscious, that he was soiled.

"Where were you before?"

"In Zapolje."

"I've been to Zapolje, too. They have a lovely church there."

"A lovely church," he repeated, slightly bewildered, looking into her eyes. And when he looked into her eyes, she laughed anew and abruptly rested her hand on his. A burst of heat came over him. He did not pull back his hand.

"How strange you are, mister. When I hear your voice or look at you, I have to laugh…And what small hands you have, much smaller than mine. And totally white!"

The blood rushed to his face and his vision clouded over. He took her hand in his and squeezed it.

"I haven't even asked you your name! We're going to be friends, so I'd like to call you by your given name!"

"My name is Tončka.—I'd like it a lot if we were friends."

"Give me your hand, Tončka. No—your lips!"

He kissed her on the mouth. On her full, hot cheeks. On her neck and on her blouse.

"Can you ever kiss! I guess you learned that in the city, sir? In Blatni Dol they aren't so supple or high-class as that. Will you be coming here every day, mister?"

"Every day!"

"Come on then! Back at the church I said to myself right away: 'Maybe he'll come to our place…I hope he comes by our place!'"

"Things must be pretty dreary for you here in Blatni Dol, with nothing but mud and darkness!"

"It's not that it's dreary, but sophisticated people seldom come here and I like having conversations with sophisticated people. They have a totally different way of talking, they bathe, and they're so…smooth. You would not even need to wear this jacket and collar; I could tell by your face that you were the stylish sort…"

"You are so child-like, Tončka!" Kačur snickered.

She set her lips firmly and looked at him incredulously.

"How so?"

"Don't take it the wrong way, Tončka. It suits you so well!—Hold on! Now I know that your name is Tončka, that you are pretty, and that I like you! Just tell me one more thing: is the innkeeper your father or your employer?"

"Neither father nor boss. I am a foster child in this house, though we are related. My aunt is an evil woman, and my uncle is an alcoholic who blows nearly everything on drink. He's going to set me up with a trousseau but nothing more."

"Are you thinking about getting married, Tončka?"

"I'd like to, indeed, but only to a fine gentleman. I'd take somebody like you!"

"Oh, Tončka!"

"What are you laughing at?"

"Because my heart is so glad. I like listening to you when you talk with such gravity, and I enjoy looking at your face when it is so singularly serious…No one could possibly be sad when you're around. My heart is all love and desire!"

"Your words are so beautiful!"

It had grown dark as they sat amidst deep shadows, their bodies tightly intertwined. The blood pounded in his cheeks; he trembled and pressed her body closer to his.

"Tončka...I'll come see you tonight..."

"Yes, come!"

"When the tavern is closed...In the night!"

"Come!"

After that they spoke no more. She lit the lamp and her cheeks were also in flames.

When he left, everything was spinning. His face and lips were burning, and sweat beaded his forehead. But, like a bolt of lightning striking in the night, he had a presentiment that now all the wraiths of Blatni Dol, leaden, filthy, had descended onto his heart. And something akin to terror hit him.

"I won't go! I was drunk! It was a spell!"

Spring was unfolding, drifting towards him on the breeze from the fields and their moist soil. The air hung heavy, saturated with intoxicating perfume. The earth woke up, and its initial breath was labored and humid; lustful, covetous dreams were in the soil. The wind, blowing in from beyond the mountains, mingled with the atmosphere in Blatni Dol and its low-lying fog banks and it was as anesthetizing and warm as a forbidden embrace.

"I will go!" What else do I have to do in Blatni Dol? Why shouldn't I have a life?"

And he failed to notice how a beautiful memory faded as the heavy nocturnal shades enveloped the whole of Blatni Dol, including him.

CHAPTER TWO

Kačur was sitting in the dismal tavern; his face was pale, crestfallen, and aging fast. The innkeeper wobbled about on drunken legs, screaming as he slammed his fist on the table.

"Such a thing will not happen in my house! My house is an honorable home! I'll drag that slut into the street by her hair, and that damned gigolo along with her!"

The innkeeper's chubby wife was standing in the doorway. Her hands were resting on her hips.

"Why are you screaming at him? He already told you what he intends to do. Leave him alone already!"

The publican was tongue-tied but fastened his witless, bloodshot eyes on Kačur.

"What is it he said?"

"Look at our old drunkard! Didn't the man just stand up and swear that he'll take her as she is, without a dowry and without a trousseau?"

The innkeeper swayed back and forth, his emaciated, unshaven face twisted into a broad grin. He stepped closer, reached out with his hand across the table, and knocked over a glass.

"If that's how it is, then so be it!"

"So be it!" Kačur responded in a hoarse voice. He gave the innkeeper's moist hand a cursory shake, found his hat, and stood up.

"Where are you off to?—A liter of wine for the table, old lady!"

Kačur waved them off, saying he had no time, and strode out of the room without saying goodbye.

In the foyer he ran into Tončka, her face streaked with tears. He was about to walk right past her without a word when he turned around and took her by the hand.

"Tončka!"

He wanted to talk, but he couldn't find the words. He was so worked up that his lips were trembling.

"Look, I mean, maybe it was too soon...too quick...too accidental...Perhaps it wasn't right.—But let it be done according to the will of Providence! Now we are bound together forever!"

"Your words are so weighty that they almost scare me. Don't you love me anymore? Is that over now?"

Something akin to rebellion and reproach had appeared in her eyes. He had never seen such an expression on her face before, and it pained him.

"I do love you, but things are different now! I swore not to leave you, to stick by you forever, because I came to you that very first evening. And that very first night. I know that something has come between us, although I myself hardly understand it. It's like a shadow, or a pit. Yet I believe, Tončka, that we can bridge this pit if we take each other firmly by the hand...Now, to be sure, this isn't our last conversation. God be with you!"

He kissed her on the cheek and walked slowly through the streets, his head hung low. He was tired and sick.

Kačur was profoundly aware that in the shortest possible time his life had been stood completely on its head. And he had been altered along with it. And the more distinctly he felt and acknowledged this change, the more clearly he could see into his past and future. He had fallen, but now he was more stable than he ever had been; a weight had fallen onto his shoulders, and with the burden his strength had grown.

He locked himself into his room but did not light the lamp. He sat down on his bed, leaned forward with his elbows on his knees, and buried his head in his hands. Images from earlier times passed before his eyes, but nary a one of them was bright; thoughts calved off from the darkness of the days to come, but nary a one of them was sweet.

...But it was only a matter of a few days, a few steps, back to the time when he was still strong and happy and preparing himself for a fight with the entire world! No sooner had the aurora of that sun disappeared—and, look! It was as if it had set forever, as if it would never reappear. That is impossible! The day is not that brief, and one's youth does not slip away so swiftly!

...If one of them, one of those weaklings, toadies, or careerists, could see him now—him, the one who had looked down on them once with disgust and disdain! Once? Heaven help me, it was yesterday! How he would turn scarlet and break out in tremors before them! How haughtily the cry-babies and lickspittles would be able to mock him to his face! You still want to educate the masses? Bring salvation to the people? Are you still working at it? Thumbing your nose at hell, and lightning, and the school board? My God, have you slacked off so quickly?"—And how was he supposed to answer them? He would hang his head and say nothing.

His insides were churning; his entire being was in the process of recoiling.

...Why do the days of glory have to be over? When, and why, had he abandoned his true self and renounced his lofty goals? Who had transformed his heart so deftly? Who had turned his thoughts so abruptly in another direction, down the precipice into the stifling valley? When had all this happened, and why?

Am I still myself, the person my mother brought into the world? Or is it somebody else sitting here in my place, thinking for me, talking and acting for me, and against me?

He was racking his brain; he was feverishly overwrought; but he adroitly avoided that dark and unpleasant issue that lay quite close at hand. Because people strain themselves the most when they can't see something, or don't want to see it. It was as if Tončka were standing there in the shadows, in the corner there behind the door. There she stood, perfectly quiet, but he turned his head to the side and nervously looked away so that he'd miss seeing her. And so his eyes gravitated to something else, but he still saw a deserted room with him and her both in it. She had encroached on his life, made herself at home there, with all her trumpery and chattels, and placed shackles on his body and his soul and all his thoughts. His earlier existence had been solitary; but now he no longer even possessed his own ideas or desires, and his wretched body, jaded and exhausted by worry and loathing, wrung out by indignation, would end up flopping about in a cess-pool.

He sighed; it was at times like this that he wished he had a friend.

"Whom should I call? To whom could I pour out my sorrows?"

He thought back to the doctor; he would have been ashamed to go to him this humiliated and afflicted. Then, all of a sudden, his colleague Ferjan appeared before his eyes from out of the obscurity: cheerful, tipsy, and noble-minded.

Kačur smiled and wrote Ferjan a long letter.

"I know he'll come!"

In the morning the priest's rotund maidservant walked into his room.

"Sir," she called out in a surly voice. "The priest sends word that you should come to him immediately!"

"I have to go to the school."

"Go see him right this instant! What is it you need to do at school?"

And she slammed the door.

Kačur made his way over to the priest's. The latter had just come from church and was changing clothes to go out to the fields.

"Mother of Mercy!" he cried when Kačur came into view. "Have you gone off your rocker?"

"What makes you say that?" asked Kačur with a smile so forced that it bordered on pathetic.

The priest smacked the floor with his boot.

"Why?" he yelled. He was so angry that the blood vessels in his forehead had swollen up and were protruding. "He asks me how I know he's gone mad? Are you getting married or not? Out with it!"

"I'm getting married!"

The priest was half-way through the process of inserting his foot in the boot. He had bent down low and was gripping the boot firmly with both hands; but he raised his head and stared silently into Kačur's face. Then his eyes returned to the boot and he finished pulling it up.

"Why should I not marry?" asked Kačur, somewhat abashedly.

"Oh, but of course! Why not?" the priest said with a smile and a nod of his head. "And you plan on having kids, too, I'll bet. A lot of kids?"

"Perhaps!" Kačur said, his face flushed.

"Maybe! So that's how it is! 'Maybe I'll have kids, or maybe I won't! Maybe they will live, or maybe they'll croak!'—Oh, you confounded urchin, you ignoramus!—How I'd love to take these boots and pelt you across the face with them!"

The priest was wheezing and his hands were quivering with rage.

"No, he hasn't lost his marbles; he's just a good-for-nothing guttersnipe! And he wants none other than the woman who doesn't come to church to pray but rather to show off her big breasts and her tasteless outfits! May God bless her! But I'm going to hit you two with a sermon, the likes of which the world has never heard!—What are you going to live on? Love? Pooh! Pooh! Pooh! When a farm-hand gets married, it's all about getting married instead of womanizing. But a teacher is even lower than a farmhand; he can't live like a lord, but he's not allowed to live like an animal. So—nothing doing!"

Kačur turned and made for the door.

"Where are you going?"

"What, is the sermon not over yet?"

The priest lowered his voice.

"Go in God's name, and do what you will! But I have to tell you one thing: I pity you."

The priest quickly finished dressing, not uttering another word. Kačur stood for a while longer on the threshold and then walked off.

"That peasant!" An enraged Kačur thought, as he left the rectory. But something bitter and oppressive remained in his chest and weighed on him more and more.

"Lord knows he meant well! And there must be a touch of truth in what he says.—To be done with this, once and for all!—Then we could rely on the Lord to guide us!"

A couple of days later, on Saturday night, Ferjan arrived on his mission of mercy. He greeted Kačur with a hearty laugh and shook his hand. But to Kačur it seemed that Ferjan's laugh was no longer as guileless as it once had been, and his face seemed rather drawn.

"So, Mr. Idealist, now you've taken the bait! Your letter to me was very wordy, but at last I did figure out that you have really gotten into a pinch and now, in your distress, you want a glimpse of a good Christian face.—So now, how did you get into this mess?"

Kačur shrugged his shoulders.

"Actually I can easily imagine how you did this to yourself.—Your room here is damned dreary! It makes me want to cry my eyes out. Come on, let's go to a pub."

They went to the mayor's place. Ferjan talked the whole way over and continued once they got there:

"You are depressed. It shows on your face. But you know what? If push comes to shove, why should you even be depressed? Until now you've been living alone, just for yourself (as you say), a free man (as you say)—but what was your life like? Miserable, for God's sake! This independence, this freedom, what did it do for you? What did you do with it? Not a damned thing…I think it's much worse for someone to be hanging from the gallows alone than for him to have a partner in suffering. You can trade glances, at least, and that counts for a lot…So, Christian man, take solace! Who's that bean-pole over there?" He pointed at the tall secretary, who immediately hurried over to their table and took a bow.

"Karel Grajžar, Municipal Secretary!"

"What?" Ferjan remarked in surprise. "Why do they have a municipal secretary in Blatni Dol? And if that's the case, explain to me right here and now why in this damned hollow there's so much darkness, cold and filth, when everywhere else in the world the sun is warming things up?"

"The sun?" The secretary arched his eyebrows. "I've never seen it."

"Because he's always plastered!" thundered the slurred voice of the Mayor from the neighboring table.

"OK, you short-legged Achilles—adieu!—Let's you and I, Kačur, get on with the matter at hand! Since you have appointed me the doctor of your distress, I ask you: do you love her or not?"

Kačur looked him in the eyes but did not answer right away.

"Well?" Ferjan said, shaking his head. "Misery is misery."

"I do love her," Kačur responded. He was staring pensively at the table. "This much is certain: I shouldn't leave her for someone else to take. For the rest of my life, I'd think about that with hurt and desire. I don't know what kind of love this is; I haven't thought about it and I don't want to! Whether she's a Madonna or a serving girl—that's not my concern! All I know is that there's neither peace, joy, nor sunshine in this love! Nonetheless it is an awesome love. And I will never vanquish it!"

Ferjan scrunched up his face; curious wrinkles of annoyance appeared; and he sat looking at Kačur's profile.

"And what's up with Minka?"

"Don't go there!" Kačur's look was forbidding.

"Ah, your sacristy!"

"Sacristy, indeed!" Kačur gave a sad smile.

"Well, here's my opinion, Kačur: this girl is infinitely preferable to a genuine love, the kind of love that the sun itself merits. You'd be in chains.—And it would be hell, and you'd go to wrack and ruin. This thing here will be easier to deal with. You'll calm down. Her tears will gall you less, and your woe will thus attenuate because you'll come at things with a cooler head...Why the wicked laugh? I only wanted to comfort you!"

Kačur drank urgently. His face was grave and his eyes clouded.

"That's cold comfort. You are basically just relating your own misfortune without intending to. In recent days my vision has become very acute...What's going on with Matilda? Has she become your bride?"

The look on Ferjan's face was half-mournful, half-droll.

"You know what? There is less tragedy than divine chastisement in my case. How is that? I'll have Satan on my heels, that's all...I'll get a beating when I drink—who cares? I used to get thrashed from time to time, and then in the morning I'd notice that it hurt; but I didn't know who had cudgeled me. Now I'll always know who's been whaling on me!—And get this: lately she's been trying to land this young doctor. I was irate, and even sick at heart, so much so that I was barely conscious of what I was saying: I hope she catches him!—She didn't pull it off, and I was furious at her, and she was furious at the doctor, so we got engaged...And now I've taken up this cross, and I'll be walking around with it the same way I walked around without it till now. You still have no idea how strong my back is.—But with you it's an entirely different matter. I don't want to scold you, but you know exactly what's going on.—And you also know why your situation is completely different."

Kačur said nothing.

"Basta!" Ferjan gave a dismissive wave. "These are melancholy discussions. I don't like to whine.—So, tell me, have you already been preaching the Gospel around Blatni Dol?"

"I haven't been preaching anything."

"I should hope not!—You won't be doing any more of that anyway, I don't think."

"If Christ Himself could come to Blatni Dol, He'd hold His tongue. Nowhere on earth have I seen people such as these: the night is so pitch black that not even a hundred suns could penetrate it. I've watched farmers in their fields as they trot along next to their livestock, with the same lazy, lumbering steps, swaying back and forth in the same oafish gait—and on their faces—believe me!—lay the same dull, immobile expression, devoid of all thoughts and feelings like the staring eyes of farm animals...Such is this heavy, cloying soddenness creeping forth from the earth; such are these shadows, hovering constantly on the soil."

"Earlier you would have brought light even into a night like this one," Ferjan remarked with a chuckle.

Kačur knew what this criticism meant. He recalled: this is exactly how one of those cry-babies or sycophants will confront you, laughing right in your face...The blood rushed to his cheeks.

"I have not given up on my goals or on myself!" he cried out with a shiver. "I have betrayed nothing and I have missed out on nothing. Later...when..."

"Just go ahead and say it!" Ferjan interjected with a hearty laugh. "Later, when you are married! That's when you'll spread the gospel! Then—how did you put it just now—then you'll start serving the people, instructing them, directing them onto the path of prosperity and progress!—And, on the basis of this kind of imbecility in your head, you want to get married?"

Kačur mopped his brow. Now his eyes revealed fewer inhibitions.

"Let it be according to God's will!—For good or ill, I brought it all on myself. But I'm sure about this much: I will not live like a beast. Not because I don't want to, but because I can't!"

"That's another matter.—Have you considered the other issues?"

"Which ones?"

"Aha, I knew it!—You'll need money! Lots of money! Where do you plan to get it?"

"I haven't thought about that at all."

"Of course you haven't.—All right, I'll see if something can't be done for you; I mean, I have experience in that. And furniture? Will she have a trousseau?"

"She won't have anything! Or at least not much."

"Holy Mother of God! You're getting into a hell of a jam.—And for all that you still want to be an evangelist?"

When they took their leave of each other the next morning, they were closer than they had ever been; by looking into the other man's eyes, each understood the other without talking.

Kačur thought: "You've already gone down this forlorn path, but I never will!"

Ferjan thought: "I've already gone down my forlorn path, and now you will, too!"

As the hour of the wedding approached, Kačur felt himself becoming more and more alienated from his bride. Slowly, but steadily, they grew apart, and Kačur grew afraid. He regarded his betrothed differently now; his view of her was cooler and more composed. Consequently he found that she had changed; when someone looks up close at a face that he or she knows well and loves, what becomes visible are tiny spots, easy to overlook, and minute wrinkles, and other unattractive features. She came stomping into his life, forced her way into his tranquil room, into his soul, and never left him alone after that. He embraced this newcomer, for he was alone and downhearted, but more and more now he feared her. He sensed ever more that she brought nothing to his life; she was simply threatening to take possession of him completely, to usurp his soul.

Sometimes Tončka stared at him for long periods, causing him to lower his eyes. She suspected what was in his heart, and it irritated her.

"He doesn't care for me anymore. He's been with me, nibbled my lips, and found that I tasted good. But now he doesn't love me. He drank his fill, got enough, and now he's off to another!"

And just as she intuited his thoughts, he intuited hers. They seldom spoke to each other, and when they did they were cold and peremptory. Sometimes they still kissed. The old passion would reawaken, and their faces would burn with heat. For an instant.

The only person in the house who was glad was the alcoholic innkeeper. He would sometimes cry out that there had never been a couple like this for ten parishes around. And sometimes, when he could no longer stand up and had to prop himself against the table, he began to weep, feeling sorry for himself and bemoaning his solitary life. He nauseated Kačur, who apprehensively sought to avoid him whenever the innkeeper came at him with his bloodshot eyes, moistened lips, and outstretched arms.

Kačur found everything that transpired between the engagement and the wedding ceremony immensely tiresome and obscene. A seamstress had moved into the inn with the family; Tončka cheered up; she moved about the rooms more briskly; her cheeks looked rosier; and a smile was on her lips. This happy face did not please Kačur, in part because it was now prettier than it had been earlier.

"Just look at how she has brightened up! The seamstress made her this happy! Her thoughts are like cigarette ashes on the table.—Blow on them and they're gone! Where there is silk, the past and future no longer exist!"

He inquired peevishly, "What's the use of such elegant stuff?"

"Allow me this one pleasure, at least! Why should I look like a serving wench when I go to the church with you?"

"The groom has no say in all this!" the innkeeper's wife added. "Go about your business!"

In his quarters one of the walls was demolished in order to create a bigger apartment for the young couple. Kačur lodged for the time being at the mayor's, who, every time he saw him, shook his head and said, "Oh, my!"

But that's all the mayor said. Grajžar also said nothing, but blinked his water eyes constantly and tightened his face again into those exquisitely strange wrinkles, half-ridiculous and half-morose. Every once in a while the mayor turned his way and nodded mutely; the tall secretary then nodded back just as silently. If Kačur was walking about outside, the farmers greeted him with a great deal less respect, almost with contempt actually, and the lads made jokes about him and stared at his back.

Kačur felt more and more confined. And an unaccustomed thought troubled his mind. He could not ward it off.

One evening as he was leaving the inn and saying goodbye to his bride in the entrance hall, he drew very close to her and said, in a low, irresolute, quavering voice:

"Tončka, don't be offended, but I have to ask you something. People are looking at me so strangely.—Of course they're idiots, but I have to ask you this to put my mind at ease!"

He stopped. She stood silently before him, looking crestfallen.

He leaned even closer to her, right up to her ear.

"Was there someone else you loved…earlier…before me?"

She retreated a step towards the wall, covered her face, and started to cry.

"Now you're starting with that already!"

His head cleared at once, and he felt ashamed. But he wasn't strong enough to take her by the hand and beg for forgiveness. Something inexplicable—like a gloomy thought or an inky shade—pulled him away.

"So then…adieu!"

He walked quickly through the streets. It was a warm, humid evening; the sky was clear; and the stars slumbered in the distance, so remote that the eye could barely locate them.

"I surely did her an injustice just now! But—ach, how despicable and nauseating we are made by this despicable, nauseating life!"

The furniture that Kačur had ordered was delivered in a large wagon.

"See there!" he said to his fiancée, as the wagon clattered past the inn on its route through the village. "Go on over and fix everything up the way you want it! I can't be bothered with it!"

"But that's supposed to be one of the things you take care of!"

She hastily tied a scarf around her neck.

"But then again I would like to see it…Come on! What's the delivery boy supposed to do by himself?"

"I don't want to. I see in it nothing but a huge debt, and a heavy burden at tax time, stacked up two fathoms high!"

He filled his glass and drank. Tončka left.

The furniture made her happy; it was from the city and very modern. She was also happy about her new clothes, and about the big stack of white linens with lace, and about the engagement itself, and the coming wedding. But tears forced their way into her eyes.

"He doesn't care for me anymore. He's very angry, and very much changed!"

And he still did not suspect that her love was now completely different as well, and that she barely touched him, her intended, and then only as if from afar.

When that lovely summer's day arrived, an unanticipated sense of pleasure made itself felt even in Kačur's heart.

"Is this really the first time the sun has shone in this mournful darkness?" he wondered as he looked out the window.

People in holiday outfits were moving through the lanes; the farmers' faces seemed brighter and friendlier, and their voices weren't as grating or hoarse as earlier, and even their gestures were no longer as lifeless or ponderous.

"I used to say: what can you do with this population? Even these people are worthy of a better life. One must only trim the wild pear tree and it will bring forth precious fruit!"

Ferjan materialized underneath his window, ready to escort the bride and give her away. He was wearing a stylish black coat. He called up towards the window:

"Are you finally going to venture out of that lousy hovel, or not?"

"At once, at once!" Kačur responded, laughing.

When he went outside, when he met people up close, he noticed their inquisitive glances, and when he entered the inn, pressing the hands of a lot of half-strangers and answering a lot of questions he did not understand, he heard laughter and the clinking of glasses—and something cast a pall over his heart again like a shadow.

Ferjan admonished him: "You cannot behave this way!"

"Just leave me alone!"

The sun beamed hot into the valley. But to Kačur it did not seem as if the sun were bright, but rather that the shadows that filled the valley had ignited. Dusty, hot fog was what he saw. Wagons rattled, bright clothing flashed, and a visage draped in a broad smile was taking shape in the sticky air above the road. The colorful crowd surged outside the church.

"Well, so he got too close to the fire," someone standing by a wagon piped up. Laughter ensued.

The priest came out to the altar, raced through the ceremony, and then looked at the two of them. He was brimming with resentment when he said:

"But I must tell the two of you, you—"

The church was full, and somebody at the door started laughing. The priest dismissed them all with a wave of his hand and turned on his heel.

"I'd rather go into this in the sacristy!"

Once in the sacristy, the priest laid both his hands on Kačur's shoulders and looked at him tartly from under his gray brows.

"I married you two, but there is no blessing on these proceedings, I'll tell you that much! I'll come to the celebration so that you two can't say anything. What happens later is a matter for the two of you, and the Lord."

He spun around and walked away.

Kačur drove away from the church with his bride, the young wife. He looked at her from the side; her face was flushed and full of happiness, and her eyes shone.

"She is happy!" he thought to himself, as bitterness crept into his heart.

A young man standing outside near the tavern removed the cigar from his mouth and shouted after their wagon: "That snot-nosed kid there decided he just had to have a fancy wedding! Well, I could've had her, that Tončka, if I had wanted her!"

"There's no truth in that!" his wife exclaimed quickly. Her voice trembled. She looked over at Kačur with fearful, lachrymose eyes.

"What the hell do I care?" Kačur replied. He was in a foul mood when he sauntered into the entrance-way.

In the reception hall, sitting at a long, decorated table, surrounded by full bottles and cheerful, noisy guests, he took a look around. Nausea erupted and spread in his insides.

"What have I gotten myself into now?" he asked himself.

Common, coarse faces, celebrating; shiftless, drunken eyes; even the priest would have been unrecognizable had it not been for his collar.

"The minute he's in Rome, he does as the Romans do!...I might well be like that someday, too!" And Kačur's heart ached.

He stood there, observing, battered by ugly thoughts, until he suddenly, incredulously, noticed that Ferjan was standing up on a table. He was giving a speech, trying to catch Kačur's eye.

"...And may God grant the Evangelist and his wife much happiness! And may the Lord provide them with many children—the more, the better!..."

Kačur took a look at Ferjan, and then at his wife, and he realized how Tončka was eyeing the orator: with a gleam in her eye and parted, heaving lips. He felt a sudden stab of shame, grabbed his glass, and downed it in one gulp.

"...And in conclusion: may God hold her in the palm of His hand, and him!" With that, the oration was finished.

A farmer got to his feet and, instead of a toast, delivered a dirty joke. The wedding guests guffawed; Tončka turned red and her laughter tolled forth like a bell.

Ferjan gave Kačur a bow.

"It's your turn, you know!"

"So what?" came Kačur's gruff reply.

"My God, I've seen weddings like this, but never a groom like you!"

Kačur stood up.

"I thank you very much for your words of friendship! I believe that my wife and I will be living in accordance with God's will for us; and for the rest of you, it is also my wish that your lives not be too terrible.—To the health of our village elder and marriage witness, and all these guests!"

Once again laughter droned throughout the hall; the assembly rose and clinked glasses all around. Ferjan was drinking a lot and his eyes were starting to glaze over.

"Hey...were you serious about that?...Are you rejoicing?"

"I was in earnest."

"Wait—I have to tell you something: I shall never marry!"

"So you've been thinking about this?"

"Not me.—She has!"

"What?"

"Oh, yes! And how! Can you imagine? It makes me sad! I wish she had beaten me black and blue instead! Now she's gone off with some beanpole of an officer. God knows where they've gotten to...Maybe she'll be back!"

Kačur got to his feet.

"Where to?" asked his wife, alarmed. "We haven't even danced yet!"

"I won't be dancing! I feel like sleeping. Dance by yourself!"

"What a way to act! Tonight?"

"It is what it is!—Really, Tončka, just stay! Ferjan will see you home! And he'll even entertain you on the dance floor. Farewell, Ferjan!"

"What in the world is wrong with you?" Ferjan wondered out loud.

Kačur was pale and haggard; he leaned on Ferjan's shoulder, stammering like a drunk.

"Only now can I see it, my friend..."

"What do you see?"

"That I've committed suicide!"

And he traced a circle around his throat and neck with his hand.

"To think that I knotted my own noose. And placed it over my own head!"

He departed and not a single guest even noticed.

The light was on in his room when he heard drunken voices below his window. They were striking up one bawdy song after another. The only voices he could actually make out were those of Ferjan and his wife.

"Ahoy there!" came Ferjan's hoarse scream. "Are you already asleep up there, you old knave? His wedding night, and he goes to bed and leaves his wife out in public!"

Kačur opened the window.

"Martin! Why did you leave?" his wife called out, her voice syrupy and half-sozzled.

"Good night, Ferjan!"

He shut the window, the door creaked, and in the distance drunken singing could be heard.

CHAPTER THREE

It was fall and Blatni Dol already lay in darkness and frost. Gray, unwelcoming light penetrated the room.

The child slept in a crib. His face was round, bright, and at peace.

"Don't yell like that when the child is asleep!" Kačur hissed. "Wait till he's awake. Then you can shout as much as you want!"

The woman's face was flushed and streaked with tears.

"So I'm not supposed to shout? I nurse the child, change his diapers, and get up with him at night! But what do you do for him? You don't lift a finger! And now you start this whole drama—we're all going to die on the street, for sure! Why do you have to do that, when you have a wife and child?"

Kačur gave her a malicious glance, picked up his hat, and walked out.

"Go then! Just go!" the woman blustered after him. She began to cry loudly. Then the child awoke and started bawling.

Kačur hurried through the muddy streets.

"Come have a look at me now, Ferjan! How you'll laugh at the Evangelist now!"

It was getting on towards evening. Kačur saw a man reeling along the row of houses. He was covered in muck and wore no hat; he was holding onto the walls but kept falling down anyway.

"Look at him—my father-in-law!" he marveled aloud and tried to move on swiftly. But the innkeeper had seen him and came staggering across the road with long strides and his arms extended.

"Is that you, Martin? Let me lean on your shoulder…I'm having a hard time walking…Come have a nightcap with me! Ach, Martin, I am old, old!"

"Go to bed, father," Martin cried out as he tried to shake him off.

"Sleep? Why?"

Swaying, he looked at him with furious red eyes.

"Because you are intoxicated."

"Who's intoxicated? I am more sober than you are! Take a look, folks!—And look here: the pretty boy wants to put me in my place."

"Go to sleep!" Kačur shook himself free and kept walking.

The proprietor took him by the arm.

"Just don't act so high and mighty, you misfit! Are you trying to get above your raising? Think you're better than all of us? Want to teach us a lesson?"

With a force that comes from drunkenness, he gave Kačur a shove that sent him reeling.

"Just go then! Do you think we're blind to the fact you don't even own the trousers on your ass?"

Kačur rushed away. The innkeeper's laugh rang out, and subsequently he took a giant stride and tipped over in the mud. Someone was watching from the window, let out a laugh, and stared after Kačur. On the corner stood a farmer, lighting his pipe and winking contentedly.

"That one there wants to stand the world on its head! He doesn't like the way we plow, the way we sow, or the way we treat our livestock. What a guy! And he wants to teach us how to read! But he'd better watch out himself!"

Kačur entered the tavern owned by the mayor. He was red in the face and had tears in his eyes.

The mayor was seated at the table, leaning far back in his chair. He was smoking a small pipe and stared at Kačur with his eyes squeezed to slits. At last, he cautiously pulled the pipe out of his mouth and spat onto the ground.

"What do you want, schoolteacher?"

"What do I want?"

The mayor's broad grin was half-scornful, half-happy at Kačur's misfortune.

"Well, now, you're planning on schooling the old folks along with the young'uns? When are you going to try it with me? Well, just go ahead. Teach me how to pour wine. Just go show the farmers how they should work their fields! Teach it to me as well! I have fields. Lots of them!"

He smiled so broadly that his entire face lit up.

His secretary sitting in the corner grimaced; he stroked his long narrow beard and kept blinking rapidly.

"Your Honor!" he called out suddenly.

The mayor twisted around in his chair.

"Your Honor, you are rather in need of some lessons. And the cane!"

"What?" the mayor fumed. He leapt up from his seat.

"*Parlez-vous français?*" [1] asked the secretary, as he stroked his beard.

"What did you say?"

"*Parlez-vous français?*"

The mayor was flabbergasted. He looked over at Kačur.

"Now he speaks French! Is there anything he can't do?" Kačur said, smiling.

"Oh, you son of a bitch!—Mica, bring him another half liter!"

Then he turned back to Kačur and grew so serious that wrinkles appeared on his face. His hair fell down over his eyes and the corners of his mouth turned down as far as his double chin.

"I'm not saying anything against you, schoolteacher. You're a smart man and so on and so forth. Nevertheless…"

He slapped his palm on his thighs.

"…Thus far we've gotten along peaceably, and we want to continue to live that way!"

"What have I done to you? Don't I leave you in peace?" Kačur rejoined.

"Heck no! You do not leave me in peace!" The mayor flew into a temper. "What do you think you're

[1] "Do you speak French?" (French in the original.)

doing with the people without my knowledge? Did you even ask me when you called them together in the schoolhouse?—I know that Samotorec cooked all that up!"

"Samotorec?"

"He wants to be mayor," the secretary announced from his corner.

"But both of you should remember one thing, teacher, and I'll tell you and that old troublemaker who has latched onto your coattails this: you won't get rid of me so fast! Him, and you too—I can buy both of you with what I have in my wallet right now."

And with that he smacked his pocket and made it jingle.

Kačur was half-enraged, half-astonished.

"Who was even thinking of that? Not a living soul! I don't even know if Samotorec was there. Maybe he was. But this isn't about politics, and it isn't about the Mayor's office! All it's about is the people learning something! That they sharpen their minds. That they see a bit farther, beyond these mountains! That's what it's about!—They need to be ordering books and subscribing to newspapers, and those men who travel around enlightening people about new ways to manage farms—they should come to Blatni Dol, too...That's what we said. Nothing more!"

The mayor looked at him mistrustfully.

"Just get this through your skull, teacher: never make a move against me! I know how it works! You've made common cause with these cottagers and tenant farmers! Why should they learn to read? And the tenant farmers who don't own the tiniest bit of land and who've at most rented a little plot—why should they learn to till the soil? I lived well when I was still selling linen and canvas and now I'm doing pretty well for myself, too. I don't want anything to change. No books, no journals, and no schoolmasters! No, I don't want that, and nobody who owns anything in Blatni Dol wants it either. Yeah, the cottagers and the roustabouts who just own their shanties—they like things like this. And why is that? Two years ago, I think it was, one fellow came and worked for the blacksmith. He could speak German. We didn't inquire about where he came from, and if we had, he would've lied to us about it. And he didn't just give the cottagers and tenant farmers lessons; he explained to them that the land doesn't only belong to those of us in possession of large estates, but to all the people on earth. And that all men and women are equal in value, whether they have money in their pocket or not. And that it is an injustice if I have ham on my table while the cottager has potatoes in their skins. This is what he taught.—And do you know what befell him in the end? Misfortune struck him, and there he lay, on the road, with his skull smashed in. It happened on the way to the parish fair, and at a parish fair there are always lots of fights, and so the gendarmes didn't concern themselves too much about who had caressed him so mercilessly. Now what do you say to that?"

Kačur stared at the mayor with glassy horror in his eyes. They mayor laughed, his double chin wobbling, and his eyes were altogether swallowed up by his chubby cheeks.

"That's what he taught them! And that's why they like such lessons. And that's also why the school was full when you called together the cottagers and the tenants. And Samotorec, that mother of all cottagers, he was there, too! You know completely well that he was in on it!"

Kačur rose to his feet, pale and trembling.

"What is that supposed to mean? What are you trying to say? Does that mean that I'll be lying in the road with a crushed skull one day?"

The mayor continued to chuckle, quietly, smugly, confidentially. His double chin wobbled and his eyes were invisible in their slits.

"Say what? I meant nothing by it! And when is the parish fair, anyway?"

Kačur left, feeling like he had had a nasty, terrifying dream. The secretary came loping after him with long strides, grabbed him by the jacket, and hissed into his ear:

"Leave him be! He is not a decent man. There's something inside of him...He's a terror!"

"Did you understand what he was trying to get across?"

"Me? Not a thing!—Let's get out of here if we can. Over to those shadows! There's someone at the window here.—What did I make of all that? Nothing! But I arrived in Blatni Dol the very day the blacksmith was left lying there with his skull shattered...Who did it? God knows? The smith is dead, so why should anybody else suffer on his account?—Stop bothering the mayor. Do not tangle with him! It'd be much better for you to clash with all your clerical and worldly masters, and with the Kaiser to boot! It's easy enough to wring someone's neck, this way or that. It's not even necessary that you do like this blacksmith and…—All he lost was his life…And what is life anyway? A handful of air—nothing more!…Alas—what am I saying? I said nothing. Absolutely nothing. Farewell!"

"Stop!" Kačur grabbed him by the arm. "You know what was up with him…that blacksmith! Out with it! I'm not letting you go."

"What?" The secretary seemed amazed; he arched his eyebrows. "What am I supposed to be in the know about? What blacksmith?"

Kačur pondered for a moment.

'Well, if that's the way it is, then why are you still in Blatni Dol? Why don't you go somewhere else? You're a free man, right?"

In the darkness he could tell that the secretary had a most queer grimace on his face.

"*Das sind Dinge, über welche um des eigenen Ansehens willen nicht gesprochen werden kann!*[2]—To put it in our language: they're looking for me! Good night, sir!"

The long, lean secretary disappeared in the night.

Kačur returned to his house. His wife set supper on the table before him; her eyes were red and her cheeks mottled. He ate hastily and then walked over to the child. He lay in the cradle, looking at him with large, clear eyes.

[2] "Those are things about which one cannot, for the sake of one's own reputation, speak." (German in the original.)

Kačur took the child in his arms and grew more relaxed and tender. He glanced about for his wife and hoped to see on her face a friendly and gentle smile as well.

She was clearing the table, keeping her head bent far over her chest while tears streamed over her face. Annoyed, he placed the baby back in his crib.

"My God, wife, what is wrong with you? At least tell me flat out what I've done to you!"

"Pah!—Here's another letter."

He walked over to the shelf and opened the letter. He didn't let his calm expression betray the tumult inside him.

"What difference does it make if I've been turned down? Only one of the ten applicants can get the position. It'll be different next time."

"You've applied at least ten times!"

"But we can wait! Are we doing so badly? Even in Blatni Dol one can make it…if need be."

The blood ran to his face; he was ashamed to humble himself this way in front of his wife; he was ashamed that he wasn't telling her how he felt. And, deep in his heart, he felt it with great and bitter force: one cannot live like this! I'd rather live in prison or exile! Just somewhere other than here, even if it means going without bread or a job. The Lord will provide! Just away from this darkness—to a place where there is sunshine!"

"We'll get by, we'll get by!" shouted his wife. "We could get by if you were like the others. I don't dare go out in public, because people look askance at me, as if I were the wife of a thief or a bandit! People already said that I'd come to regret this. Why are you spreading strife among the people? Why are you fraternizing with servants and tenant farmers and going about inviting them to meetings? You get in a huddle and plot like a band of thieves that fears the light of day.—"You ought to be ashamed!'—That's what Mrs. Kolarin said, and Lovrač said: 'He shouldn't be seen in the pub on Sundays!'—Otherwise I could go to church like lady. But now I go like a leper!"

Her speech became ever faster and louder. The child, watching her from the crib, started to cry.

Kačur went over to his wife and grabbed her hard by the hand.

"Tončka, listen! Don't talk that way!—They've told you themselves how much they hate me, how they avoid me, spit on me in secret and in public, and now you are reproaching me, too! Even though I am fond of you, and you know me! Do you know why they're mad at me? Because I want what's good for them, because I want them to live better than they have till now, and to have more dignity! But they stay mad at me, cuss at me like a thief, and threaten me as if I were a fire-bug. But soon it will be different. Soon the time will come when they'll be grateful to me and they'll love me!—But till that happens, Tončka, you at least should want to be with me! Don't you think ill of me, too! If someone I barely know hates me and disavows me, the pain is slight; I avoid him or her; I'm not tied to that person. But we two are chained to each other, in perpetuity, and my pain and horror would drive me to despair if you were to come to hate me, too, if your face were always tearstained like this, if no friendly words ever came out of your mouth.

So, since we are chained to each other, wrap your arms around me and hold me tight!"

His cheeks were on fire, while her eyes remained cool and calm.

"Those are just words! Of course I love you; you are my husband! But—why do you have to get involved in other people's troubles? What do you need with these farmhands? Why did they call upon you?—I know already; people told me. Because you sow strife among the people, since you didn't get a better job! And you were even transferred here to Blatni Dol for the same reasons. But at the time, before the wedding, you didn't say anything about it to me! You kept silent about such things!"

Kačur was boiling inside; he wanted to jump her and bash her in the face with his fist. He shook. His eyes narrowed, spraying rage.

"Shut up!" he screamed.

She just looked at him.

"Shut up!" he said once more, this time quietly through clenched teeth.

"They're having another go at it," someone said with a guffaw under their window.

Kačur went into the next room, slammed the door, and didn't reappear till morning. Until late at night he could hear his wife's sobbing and the squeaking of the crib on its hinges. Wearily he laid his head on his hands and fell asleep at the table. Between dreaming and waking, he thought of the blacksmith who was left lying on the road with his brains knocked out...Here he was, standing, not lying, in the middle of the road, bolt upright in blazing glory. His face was earnest and pale but had a thin rivulet of blood running into one eye. Kačur moved towards him, and the smith's face became more and more serious and threatening and severe. That's when Kačur saw that the smith was not alone. They were standing behind him like shadows, one next to another, in a long, long row; they were pale and all of them had blood flowing across their foreheads, over their eyes. "Where to?" asked the smith. "To your house," Kačur answered "To the home of you and your family!" "Not to my house! Your line is over there!" Kačur looked around and saw a most singular procession. At its head walked his father-in-law, drunk and bedraggled, and there was Ferjan with his stovepipe hat. They were supporting each other by the shoulders, and they were weaving back and forth. And behind them staggered oddly masked shadows one after the other, in a long, snaking row, with thin, hollow, snarling faces. Kačur wailed in horror—and he joined them, seeing himself in their bloody, torpid eyes.

"I was lying in an awkward position. That explains these stupid dreams!"

He lay down, but his head was throbbing and he wasn't able to sleep for a long time...When he finally dozed off, he saw the provincial school inspector, whom he had never met before. He was a tall, stately gentleman with a beard so long it extended to his belt. Kačur stood before him in strange attire. In the foyer he had removed his shoes, as he thought necessary, and rolled his trouser legs halfway up. Then, slipping and sliding on his naked knees, he went up the stairs, slowly and painfully—and then moved all through the long passages. Thus he appeared before the inspector in a new black jacket, top-hat in hand, barefoot, the pants legs turned up and his knees worse for the wear. The inspector glanced at him and waved slightly with his white hand; Kačur knelt down and waited. Once again the inspector extended his hand and handed him a decree, very white and very large. Kačur approached the inspector, still on his knees, kissed his hand, and accepted the decree. On it was written that Martin Kačur had been appointed teacher in Zapolje, but on one condition: that he show up after lunch and supper each and every day with a toothpick to clean the teeth of the headmaster, the priest, the mayor, and all the other members of the local school board.

Kačur woke up in a foul mood. Looking out the window, he saw that it was dawning on the other side of the mountains.

His wife brought him some coffee.

"Go on alone to church...We don't have to go together. "

Kačur looked at her silently.

"She would repudiate me for a silk handkerchief," he laughed. "And yesterday I still thought she'd comfort me....that she'd be my guardian angel."

He laughed harder, went through the other room, kissed the baby on the cheeks, and set out for church.

As he met villagers along the way, and then when he stood by the door of the sacristy and looked around inside the church, he sensed grim, devastating looks. "He's the one who would sow discord among the people! That ignoramus! He wants to teach us lessons and put us in our place! The bum who's eating up our good bread!"

Kačur did not lower his eyes, but his face stung and he felt his legs trembling, more from anger than fear.

After mass, the priest signaled to him with a nod of his head and strode swiftly ahead of him towards the rectory.

"He won't accuse me of anything—not him, who once taught others how to sing!" Such were Kačur's thoughts as he walked over. When he saw the man in his frayed robe before him, lumbering, uncouth, and rustic, Kačur had to think of how the priest had looked to him on that first day, shoveling manure in his shirtsleeves, with his pants rolled up and his feet wrapped in burlap. It struck Kačur as more ludicrous than humiliating to be following the priest around like an altar boy, harboring hopes of hearing wise, high-flying, hortatory words come from the other man's mouth.

"Well, even the mayor, that scoundrel, preached at me!" And a smile spread across his face.

The priest took off his cassock and turned to Kačur.

"You know what, teacher? I don't like this!"

Kačur gave him an astounded, inquisitive look.

"I don't like it and it's not what I want!" said the priest again, louder this time. "As long as I live—no! Thereafter you can do what you want! But you are married, and you have a child, no? Isn't that enough for you?"

As he stood there, he sipped the coffee that had been placed on the table by the stocky maid. He cast Kačur a cold, vexed glance.

"Let's be perfectly clear here: what madness impelled you to start agitating among the people, when you are not even one of them? Don't mess with them! These people belong to me. Mark it well: Blatni Dol belongs to me..."

"I don't want to take it from you."

"Silence! Hear me out!"

The priest had flown into a rage. His eyes were sparking beneath the gray brows, while on his forehead the veins swelled. He turned his back on Kačur and kept drinking his coffee.

When he turned around again, his face was more composed and his voice quieter:

"Have a seat. It's easier to talk with each other that way!—I was saying that Blatni Dol belongs to me. Actually that's only half the truth; I belong to it as well.—I have turned into a farmer, and I'm half feral, and that makes it possible to live here in this atmosphere, here among these types. It happened gradually; I was half-forced into joining them, and I did so half-voluntarily. But I did it so thoroughly that now I cannot go back. Never again! And if I had resisted back then—of what use would that have been? I wouldn't be standing in the fields but long since rotting underneath them. I would have left no attractive memories of myself behind—as it will be now, when I die someday.—That's how it is. They're in me and I'm in them! I give them the mass, and they give me the collect. I bawl them out as much as I please, and I leave them to their habits and narrow-mindedness. I am one of them in my life and in my end. Like them I do not concern myself with the external world, and I don't like it; I stick to the old ways and I hate all that is foreign to us. That's why they like me.

That's why they'll grieve for me when I'm gone.—And then you came along, an unknown young man, and therefore unwelcome in everyone's eyes. And now you have already started mingling with these folks, teaching them God knows what, how they subscribe to newspapers in which God only knows what all's written...to incite the cottagers against the property owners, and the tenants against the farmers. No, no—be quiet! I will not put up with that. I won't abide it!"

He had gotten so worked up that his hands were shaking.

"Think carefully about what you are doing! I've been living in peace for some twenty long years now! You've begun to splash around in these peaceful waters.—And where will the waves push you now? And me? You are young, so out you go into the world. But what will become of me, the old man? If Blatni Dol were to change before my eyes, over night, then what would I do in this foreign land? I would no longer have a home!—Consider this well, and do not count on my being a gentle man. Goodbye!"

"He is not a gentle man," thought Kačur as he recalled the priest's parting look.

He walked around the room with his head lowered and his arms folded across his chest.

"My knees trembled when I stood in front of the priest, too. I could feel it plain as day. But it wasn't anger; it was fear. Where else do I need to travel in order to see how low I've sunk in this place? What kind of shadows are these, if it seems to me that a heavenly sun was shining back in Zapolje? What kind of emptiness must I be carrying around in my heart for me to desire Minka and her black eyes—that contain no love! Oh, this faintheartedness!"

He moved to the window, dejected, pensive, his head heavy and his brow hot. A farmer came along the street, looked up at the window with a cold, hateful expression, and walked on by with no greeting. Sullenly Kačur turned away from the window.

"There's nothing bad about what I had in mind, right? But it was also nothing great! Would that it were at least something big that would be worth suffering and pain. Then you could go out and stand up to them and say: take your best shot! But this way it's as if you'd been condemned to death on account of a sneeze! Therefore, why sneeze if it's not an absolute necessity?"

He halted in the center of the room, a contemptuous, dismissive smile on his lips; it was as if he had caught sight of a thief whose identity he had long known; he thought back to his dream, to the school inspector and his bare feet, and he laughed out loud.

"Such is life! If a man is a coward, he can always readily prove how necessary, how logical, and how reasonable cowardice is. It doesn't even remain cowardice in his mind! He only has to lay it all out in the proper order, tot it up on his fingers, and speak forcefully. Today, this very hour, we need to be holding the inaugural meeting of the cultural association.[3] So, is this an impor-

[3] An element of early civil society in Slovenia, growing popular in the 1860s, and sometimes rendered as "reading room." They combined the functions of those small, informal libraries emphasiz-

tant matter or not? It's not important: nobody on the planet cares, no newspaper will report on it, and no poet will sing of it! Is it of any use, and to whom? It's controversial; there's no doubt about that! I, for one, consider it useful, while the mayor on the other hand does not. The priest shares the mayor's opinion. The farmers aren't speaking out for one side or the other; time will tell. And so is this idea harmful? Yes! To me! I'm turning my wife into an enemy, and the priest, the mayor, and everybody else who doesn't share my opinions. With harder work it would still amount to nothing. Maybe I'd also end up lying in the road one day with my head split open! This is a den of thieves. And the mayor is not a good man, and the priest asserts that he himself isn't one, either! But the question remains: is it my duty to go out there and establish the cultural association? No!—Has anyone asked this of me? Nobody! Therefore, am I obliged to go? No!"

He sat down at the table and buried his face in his hands.

"Oh, God! And to think that there was once a soul in this rotten flesh!"[4]

His red eyes burned but emitted no tears. His face resembled that of a consumptive: haggard, elongated, gaunt.

ing practical and political information with the functions of a programming agency for folklore, agricultural extension, the cultivation of the use of the Slovene language, and the arts. Historians usually refer to these groups as *čitalnice*, though the term Cankar uses is the related *izobraževalno društvo* ("educational society").

[4] The reader might be reminded here of *Hamlet*, Act 1, Scene 2.

"So be it! I have no right!... My son will be different...!"

He shuddered as soon as the thought of his son's being "different" crossed his mind. A powerful sense of shame befell him.

He stood up fast, pulled on his jacket, and left the room.

"Where are you off to?" his wife asked. Her face was flushed and her eyes were sparkling and defiant. He stood there, not daring to keep moving, a child's rictus on his quavering lips.

"Let me guess: you think it's not necessary?"

"Just stay here!" she rejoined in a harsh voice. "But if you think—then there's the door. Use it! But then I'll be leaving with the child, too. Somewhere."

Kačur walked back into the room.

"So it's come to this," he thought. "Now the die is cast! This is when I would open the door and go out among them. Right this instant. Maybe Samotorec will also be there. The mayor said he was at the meeting I called. And maybe that farmer, so poorly dressed and overjoyed that he was going to learn how to read...in his old age...And the farm hand who doesn't like Germanizers and wants to get books through me..."

Slowly he took off his jacket and lay down on the bed.

"It's already too late...They are already waiting...They'll be looking around: 'Why isn't he here?...When he said he'd come...'"

He sat up a little in the bed.

"But can't I do it another time?...Later? I can talk my way out of it: I had no time...I was sick.. Yes...sick, deathly ill!"

Below his window he heard voices; farmers were walking past and never before had he listened more carefully.

"He was afraid!"

"He won't make fools of us again! He's going to pay for this."

Kačur leapt up from the bed and lurched across the room. He threw on his jacket and snapped up his hat.

"Where to now?" His wife was looking at him.

"Drinking."

"Oh, feel free to go drinking…"

He pressed ahead through the streets, making eye contact with no one until he turned in at the mayor's tavern.

"Wine!" he called out.

"What's up? In such a festive mood?" The mayor was astonished.

"Festive?—Where is that spider? Where's that secretary, the one with information about who split that blacksmith's skull open?—Here, drink with me!"

At midnight he made his reeling, singing way back home. He threw the door wide open and burst into the room.

PART III

CHAPTER ONE

Underneath a set of gentle, wave-like hills clad in a growth of bushes and small trees, and laced with long clearings, a large village unfolded. The settlement, Lazi, lay spread over bottomland, hill-tops, and slopes. By a stream in the green valley, the tall, white houses pressed closely against each other. But the higher the roads led, and the more they snaked around, the more the huts and cottages avoided each other and the lower and more modest their shapes became.

A cumbersome wagon rocked slowly along the main road. There was only a tired-looking nag hitched to it, and the coachman, a spleenish old man, was ruthlessly working over its back with a whip. It was morning. The amber clearings on the hills were brightly lit by the sun, the last plumes of fog had melted away in the open sky, and the fragrance of freshness came streaming out of the cut meadows. A scythe was being sharpened in the distance, and across the fields white kerchiefs beckoned. A sickle was being lifted into the air, where it flamed in the sunshine. There was a magnificent atmosphere of peace, solemn and benign, beneath the wide heavens.

Kačur's family was seated in the wagon amongst a considerable number of crates and boxes. Ten-year old Tone and Francka, who was seven, were propped against their father; both were asleep. A child of three lay in the woman's lap, his thin little arms embracing his mother as he slept. He was as feeble as an infant, with an undersized face that was gray and sickly.

"Cover him up!" Kačur said in a quiet voice. "This morning air is nippy." And he gave his son and daughter a gentle squeeze.

The woman looked at him as if his voice had come to her in a dream. Her eyes were fixed on distant horizons, and her thoughts lingered in some far-off place as well.

Both of them wore outfits that were partly fashionable and partly rustic. You could tell that their clothes had gone through many washings and as much mending and patching as they could stand. Their fabric had faded; their cut was old-fashioned; the woman had glass earrings that flashed in the sun. She also wore a gold bracelet on her arm and a large brooch of ivory around her neck. The brooch had pictures of a male and female dove billing with each other. Her face had not aged and was as round and smooth as ever. Yet there was something common about it, something crude, and something cold and derisive in her eyes. Something was written on that face: that she had known *weltschmerz*, and had submitted without demur to the existence that the fates had held in store for her since time immemorial. Her body was quite powerful; her breasts were large. She had tied a colorful shawl around her head. Her ironed locks were combed down over her forehead in a juvenile, coquettish way. She had also attached a big clutch of carnations to her bosom.

Kačur sat farther back in the wagon, erect, tall, and slender. His suit was too big for him; its cloth was rubbed smooth and thin, and at the elbows and in spots on his back it was worn through. A long bony neck protruded from the low collar of his shirt, and his arms were equally long and bony. On his face the bones stood out as prominently as if he were a TB patient. His cheeks were overgrown with a long, ragged beard, and his eyes were dull, bloodshot in the corners. He had pushed his stiff, round hat with its broad brim far back over the nape of his neck and was looking out at the countryside.

"Wife! Look at that village! There's sun! This is where we're going to live now."

The woman did not reply, because her thoughts were far, far away.

"This is where I will live now," thought Kačur, as something beautiful, tender—something revived from the distant past—filled his heart. He cast his eyes up to the sky, up to that bright sea. He looked out over the expansive fields, at those bright kerchiefs flashing in the morn, and at the village, beckoned and gleaming in the distance.

"To live!—Once I did not know what that meant! Now at last I'll be able to find enjoyment—especially in every luminous ray of light!—Earlier, when I had nothing, I squandered things instead of nourishing myself. I showed up in Zapolje as a wastrel—showed up in sunshine exactly as gorgeous as this—and I paid no attention to it!"

"I was young," he sighed. For a moment his heart was engulfed by an almost unconscious longing for his youth.

The wagon rattled over the gravel-covered road. Tone woke up, glancing around in awe, his eyes wide-open but bleary. Kačur caressed his warm cheeks and held him close.

"Sleep on, little man! We'll soon be home!"

Tone, fatigued after the long trip and drugged by the morning air, shut his eyes at once and went back to sleep.

"Now my youth is here…a three-fold youth!"

He looked over at his wife, hungry for a kind look.

"Aren't you glad that we have finally escaped from that prison? Just take a look at this country: this is no Blatni Dol!"

His eyes contained the child-like joy of a prisoner who is finally seeing the sun after many long years, the open sky and the abundant sunshine. But her eyes held reproach, cold and silent: "This could have happened earlier."

A chill passed over him when he thought back to the prison, the heavy doors of which had just closed behind him, and to the lateness of the hour in which he found himself liberated. The diseased, poisonous air still clung to his clothes, and the shadows still streaked his face and emotions. His eyes had still not gotten accustomed to the sunlight, and his legs would still be uncertain when he walked over free earth.

Kačur was bowled over by horror: in this sunshine he saw an even blacker darkness. Over there, far beyond those mountains, the prison stood in its lowering pit. The sun had never shone on it. The damp, noxious shadows had never stirred or risen…He had entered this prison and defended himself with desperate force. With listless fists he had pounded on the iron portal; his lunatic hope had been to shove apart the mighty walls. Weary, fearful, growing weak—he let his head sink onto his chest. His back buckled and his arms hung limply at his sides... Ten years of loathing, oppressive poverty, humiliating, abject affliction.

His senses had dulled, like those of a prisoner, and he was barely conscious of how he had gradually grown used to the prison; of how the squalor and misery became his daily bread and the very air he inhaled; of how hope quietly perished in his heart. It seemed just, and reasonable, that they spurned him in request after request; he only kept writing them out of habit, in the same way he looked over notebooks in school and corrected the assignments in them. He had befriended the shadows, and the damp, stifling fogs creeping out of the heavy soil. He had conversed with the people who had at first been scornful and hostile, and subsequently their faces had ceased to seem beastlike and their eyes soulless. He fraternized with the priest, and they talked shop about the harvest, weddings, the sudden death of the chief cottager Samotorec—who had stolen grain from the drying racks[1] and oxen from people's teams—and

[1] The Slovene word is *kozolec* (singular) and denotes a tall, latticed, wooden frame with a roof. The *kozolec* is emblematic of Slovene rural life.

they discussed the war against the Turks, the Italian campaigns, and the new conflicts that would be breaking out as soon as this coming spring. He spoke German with the mayor and Italian with the secretary, and he went boozing with all of them, coming home drunk and debauched late at night. At home he quarreled with his wife and slapped her around.—But no one stopped on the street any more or looked reproachfully up at his window, because this was completely normal and very much the way it should be—bickering with the wife, hitting her—at least this meant he wasn't putting on airs!

He ground his teeth as he looked back into the darkness and saw the big, gloomy room, and his wife before him, her neck and arms bare, with her flushed face, and her eyes sparkling with malice...and there he was, bent over her, quaking with fury and spite, his fists clenched and raised... "Take that! And that!" and her shrill squawk of a voice with its "Nail me! Keep it up! Damn you!"

It took a great effort, but he tore himself away from these reminiscences. He was shuddering, as if that had all happened just yesterday, or this very hour.

So then salvation had come, but when it came he was depressed and frightened. This heart of his was no longer capable of joy; it had been too deeply debased, and too effectively stuffed with garbage. A great restlessness gripped him. He had burrowed so deeply into the shadows that he was reeling. He could no longer feel solid ground beneath his feet. When it came, after such a long period of expectation, so long desired, it was no longer even welcome... "Where will the waves carry me? What's going to become of me now that I'm an old man?" That's what the priest had said, that master and slave of Blatni Dol... Kačur was afraid to leave the prison that he had gotten used to.—Can these eyes, so much altered in the darkness, still tolerate the light?... The first great anxiety passed, the first fears, and hope awakened. His eyes could see again, were beginning to distinguish again between light and shadow, and more and more he felt the urge to dash from the night into sunshine, into the fresh morning. The closer the time of departure drew, the colder the faces around him became; no one held out a hand in friendly farewell, and he extended his hand to no one, either...

As the wagon teetered through Lazi, the sun's light was bright on the tall, white-washed residences. Two young officials were standing in front of the courthouse. They marveled at the towering load on the wagon, laughed, and then disappeared into the building. Shortly thereafter a window opened and a bearded face appeared.

Kačur sat up straight, smoothed down his hair and beard, and tugged his tie back into place. His wife fixed her shawl and used her comb to coax her curls down farther towards her eyebrows.

"Stop up there, in front of Šimon's house!" Kačur called to the driver. "It must be right by the school."

"I know, I know!" the coachman shot back. He goaded the horse forward.

"How wide the street is. And how clean!" Kačur surveyed the area. "Back there you saw more dust and mud than this inside the school, and the church, too!"

His wife sullenly cut him short. "We'll see soon enough just what it's like. All right, kids, it's time to open those eyes."

"Hey, Tone!" Kačur said, gently shaking the boy.

Both of them, Tone and Francka, opened their eyes at the same moment.

Tone's jaw dropped at the bright white buildings standing by the road, at the gardens in which large silver balls were shining, and at the fields, green and gold, gleaming lustrously behind the houses and gardens. And all these things, houses, gardens, and fields, were reflected in his marveling eyes.

Soon their furniture stood in two inviting, sunbathed rooms. But it was all haphazardly arranged and still extremely dusty.

"First of all, this dust has got to go!" Kačur exclaimed. "It's from Blatni Dol!"

They worked at arranging the apartment until evening, when they were both worn out and sweaty. Behind the building was a small garden. It had a tall apple tree in the middle, with a lot of shade and a bench underneath. A couple of yellow apples hung among the turning leaves. The children romped through the garden, which seemed to them huge and infinitely beautiful.

When night fell, Kačur and his wife went out to the garden. They sat down at the bench under the apple tree.

He took her hand and felt mellow and happy inside. As he thought back to those distant times, it seemed to him that they were knocking at his door again, where he faced them with eyes that were still largely distrusting and damp with tears.

"Tončka!" He leaned towards her. "This is a new life, and it will be totally different!...We'll be fond of each other, like we were earlier."

He put his arms around her and pressed her body to his.

"Go on, you goof-ball!" she laughed. But she remained in his embrace. They sat there in the dark, in the deep shadows underneath the apple tree, like on that first evening in the tavern, with their trembling, incandescent faces.

Kačur walked over to the school to greet his colleagues. He wore his long, old-fashioned, shabby coat and the equally old-fashioned broad-brimmed hat, and he had a long black tie around his neck. The school was so clean and bright and the scorching morning sun poured so unstintingly into the large windows that it dazzled Kačur's eyes. A clutch of cheerful young people was standing on the fresh sand in front of the gates, engaged in a vigorous discussion.

Kačur swept his hat from his head in a wide arc, and he bowed deeply.

A young man greeted him: "You've also just arrived? I saw your procession yesterday." He seemed petulant and had a thin moustache that was twisted upwards.

An older man, earnest and sturdy, held out his hand: "Welcome! I'm Jerin. I teach here!" He peered closely into Kačur's face and then chuckled. "God knows you must not have had patronage. Your career has advanced slowly."

"I have truly grown old!" Kačur laughed with embarrassment. "I have indeed advanced slowly, but for the most part I have myself to blame for it!"

"You are very humble," Jerin rejoined rather sarcastically. He turned his back on Kačur, while the young teacher with the petulant expression laughed out loud.

"Look here! It's my fault!"

A third man standing there in their group was saying nothing, and he looked at Kačur with bleary, reddened eyes. His beardless face was full of furrows and looked aged. Now it was Kačur's turn to peer closely into his face; it seemed that he had seen him somewhere before.

"Aren't you the excise officer in training? From Zapolje?"

"That's me!" the man replied drowsily. Still earning my stripes!"

The young teacher laughed. "And he follows that Matilda around like a puppy on a leash. He has wandered through half of our Slovene homeland and several German-speaking provinces with her."

"Matilda is here?" asked Kačur, his surprise so great it bordered on fright.

Brisk footsteps announced someone's progress down the stairs. A woman's voice rang out—and there was Matilda, walking out of the foyer. She studied Kačur's face up close,

She studied Kačur's face, folded her arms, and exclaimed: "Sweet Jesus! It's our evangelist!"

"Oh, for heaven's sake, not that..." Kačur said, waving his hands in protest. He laughed amidst his colossal discomfiture. "What does all matter? No use crying over spilt milk! Since then I've aged a lot…gotten married...had children."

She gaped at him, at his narrow, drawn face with all its wrinkles, the sparse beard stuck to his cheeks, his spiritless and weary eyes—at his whole bowed and broken body.

"It's just not possible…"

Kačur shrugged.

"Should a person stay obtuse forever? It harmed me quite enough! I almost waited too long to see the light."

"And to think I was once in love with you...I have to tell you this now: you have aged so terribly much!"

Kačur was annoyed by this conversation, and so he turned his attention to Jerin.

"I would like to call on the headmaster...Where is his office, anyway?"

"Upstairs," Jerin replied coolly. "He'll be coming by anyway. Why do you want to go see him?"

"I was thinking it'd be proper for me to pay him a—"

"—Whatever!"

A tall old man with a stoop and heavy tread came through the foyer. He was smooth-shaven, with a red face and snow-white hair. He had so much stuff in his pockets that they bulged noticeably. In his right hand he carried a gnarled, curved walking-stick, in the left an azure handkerchief. He smiled genially, waved the handkerchief, and nodded his head, greeting each of them in turn.

Kačur made a grand bow and was about to start speaking, when the director nodded, waved his cloth, and kept walking.

"Will you be at Gašperin's place tonight? Our tavern?" Matilda asked. "We'll strike up a song in honor of your arrival!"

"I'll be there!" Kačur pledged absorbed in thought. All the faces he had seen, all the words he had listened to—it was all so hard to reconcile with this radiant sunshine, these broad, free fields, and these refulgent buildings. He was left disturbed and uneasy.

"Where could I find the mayor?" he inquired further.

"What do you want with the mayor?" Jerin wondered out loud.

Kačur felt ashamed, for reasons he didn't understand. He could only stammer: "It would perhaps be appropriate..."

"Well, if you think so...He's over there!" Jerin pointed and continued: "The big white house on the main street. The one with the nice garden...Goodbye!"

Kačur tipped his hat, bowed with a complaisant grin, and headed over with urgent, undersized steps. He waddled a little and his feet splayed out in the manner of the faint-hearted.

"What a geek!" the haughty teacher said behind his back, loud enough for him to hear.

But he did not turn around; he just hurried on. The baggy, threadbare coat billowed around him and its tails fluttered in the wind.

"Forgive him, Father," he thought. "What does he know, the greenhorn? He has no wife and no children! May he never experience what it means to try to stand up straight when you are carrying a cross on your back with your knees trembling...I've landed in a nice little nest, a warm one, and now I'm just going to make a beeline for a quiet corner!"

He smiled to himself. The sun was blazing right into his face, making him blink.

"This is tough...Out of the night directly into the splendor of day…"

He entered the capacious, well-lit foyer and stopped before a tall glass door. No one was in sight. He didn't dare open it and also didn't know where he should knock. A maidservant came out of a low side entrance, perhaps from the cellar; she had a basket and bottles in her hands.

"Is the mayor home?" Kačur asked timorously.

"They're at home!" the maid said brusquely as she pushed the glass barrier open.

"What do you need?" she blurted out, turning around on the threshold.

"I am the new teacher..."

"I'll let the parlor maid know!"

She slammed the door and vanished; Kačur waited.

He looked around in the entrance hall. "How elegant everything is here!"

He heard footsteps and his body tautened. A slender man with a black beard opened the door from within and strode out into the entrance hall.

"Come on over here!" He smiled at Kačur, who stood there with his hat in his hand, bowing.

"Do put your hat back on!"

"Your Honor...my name is Martin Kačur. I'm the teacher. Just yesterday I arrived in this beautiful spot...and I will take pains...cause you...zero scandal."

The mayor laughed and held out his hand to shake Kačur's.

"Why should you be a source of scandal to us?...Seems to me you're a clown!"

"No!" Kačur recoiled. "I'm not a clown...Seriously, your Honor...and scrupulously. . .I will carry out my sacred duties...and I will not mess around with things that...that do not fall within the scope of activity of...no politics..."

The smile vanished from the mayor's face and his black eyes. He scrutinized Kačur closely, gravely, from under his bushy eyebrows.

"What does that matter to me? Do you consider me an informer? A teacher is every bit as free as any other person; you do what you consider right!...Sycophants don't make the best people!"

He gave him his hand, pulled it back abruptly, and walked off.

A depressed and anxious Kačur went home. The light of midday pinned him to the ground; his eyes ached whenever he looked at the fields, interwoven with restless glittering beams, as if the sun were sewing kernels of gold and silver. At the parish church, the bells of noon began tolling, and the droning, monotone answers came from the outlying chapels.

Kačur felt pain and dread in his gut.

"The priest said that it's too late, that he would be a foreigner, despised and ridiculous, if he were to betake himself to a brighter locale now..."

And then it transpired that Kačur, with pain and horror in his heart, wished he were back in Blatni Dol...wished to go back to those damp, stale shadows...where the human sleeps...where it was quiet, with nothing stirring...like in a tomb...

"Are you already drunk again?" With these words his wife welcomed him home.

The children stared at him, their eyes wide and fearful, the same way they did whenever he came home without his hat, shaking and filthy.

He dropped down at the table and put his head in his hands.

"This world is totally different, woman!"

She put food down at his place.

"Of course it's different. Thank God for that!"

Kačur raised his face and looked in amazement at his wife. She was more beautiful than ever, sensuous, shapely, eyes aglow.

"Don't you ever wish you could go to Blatni Dol?" Kačur asked, letting a wry, almost reproachful smile cross his face.

"Don't tell me that's what you want to do! There probably aren't the right drinking buddies for you here, eh?"

"O, Tončka, you—why am I even talking with you? It's like talking to a stone!"

"Look at how sullen you are already, and you haven't even been to the tavern....You know what, Kačur? At some point we are going to have to put a little effort into our clothes. I can't go to church a second week dressed like this! Their way of dress is so different here that I'm embarrassed!"

"How are we going to afford it?"

"We don't have to eat meat every day!"

"You've settled in quickly, Tončka! And you have forgotten Blatni Dol fast! Back there, silk wasn't necessary!"

"Who was pushing us to move on? And who was it who kept saying that I was going to be a lady? A beautiful lady! A dapper gentleman!"

Kačur was speechless. The sun shone into the room with powerful rays, and this light made him choke; he was afraid, just as he had once been afraid of the shadows in Blatni Dol. In this light he perceived himself to be a foreigner, frail, timid, and a stranger to his wife, who drank in huge gulps of the light until it radiated from her face and eyes.

That evening he sallied forth to Gašperin's.

When he entered the tavern, the room was already smoky, and a large party was seated around the table: a couple of young government clerks, one of whom was the somnolent finance officer; the two teachers; Matilda, wearing a flirtatious dress with short, lacy sleeves; another teacher, who was a young, skinny, bashful girl with big eyes; and the elderly, chatty wife of the freight forwarding agent. They gave Kačur a clamorous greeting and seated him between the narcoleptic finance officer and the unassertive teacher.

In the thick air of the inn, with its tobacco smoke and dim lamplight, Kačur immediately felt more at home. He sipped his wine, and it tasted good; after that, he surveyed the company.

Across from him sat a tall, handsome fellow with curly, wheat-colored hair; he had very smooth, soft skin and a sneer on his lips; he watched Kačur with his uncanny, watery eyes but looked away when Kačur's gaze met his.

One could tell that Jerin had already drunk a fair amount, owing to the powerful, imperious tone in his voice; even Matilda was laughing uninhibitedly, with her eyes starting to glaze; the finance man slumbered.

"We've been talking about you, Mr. Kačur, the revolutionary in retirement!" Matilda said with a chuckle. "Where have you been holed up that they let you get so skinny?"

"I've grown old. Aging!" And Kačur smiled in response. He took a drink. "A person gets old and comes to know other concerns and hardships and then he or she no longer feels like playing the fool…"

"Shall I tell you something, Kačur? You are dreary, quite dreary, and boring!"

She turned to face Jerin.

"Can you believe that they persecuted this person? Because he defied the authorities? Because he messed around with politics, organizing meetings and agitating among the people..."

Kačur shook his head and held up both hands in protest.

"No, no, no! What is this supposed to mean? I did not incite anyone! I organized nothing! I never horsed around with politics and I will not do so now!...I would prefer it if you all would not...get caught...that you all should toy with me...to my detriment...I do not care about anything, absolutely nothing at all!"

"Phooey!" cried Jerin. "Did you hear him? He's afraid that we are going to...oh, you damn sissy! So what are we, spies? And what would be gained by spying on a chicken like you? He doesn't even dare to wipe his nose when the superintendent is in the vicinity!—And they'd want to dragoon him?"

Matilda began to feel sorry for him.

"The times were different then."

"So what? Different times!" Jerin exclaimed fiercely. "He should've hanged himself once he saw that he could no longer live an honorable life! There were enough of them who did that!—The way he lives now brings disgrace on himself and dishonor to others!"

Kačur was drinking fast; the smile never left his lips.

"Just try it...I won't let myself be trapped! And I shan't quarrel with you...No temper! Ten years in prison...A person doesn't steal after that. Submissive instead...cautious."

He glanced across the table and noticed that the young man with the curly blond hair was already gone. Matilda's expression was cross but contemplative. The civil servant with a goatee was entertaining the spindly teacher, who was seated at Kačur's side; he was whispering sweet nothings to her, as she smiled and blushed. The trainee from finance was snoring now, his head upon the table. The forwarding agent's wife was going off on some long story to which no one was listening.

"Why the hell are you alive, if you take no interest in anything on the planet?" Jerin asked.

"I have my wife and children. And my wine!"

"Oh, so miserable!" And Jerin sighed.

This ripped a hole in Kačur's heart. His hand trembled when he raised his glass. The wine had gone to his head. There was fog before his eyes, and when he looked into the fog he could see Jerin's face—which seemed familiar to him from an earlier time. He held out his hand and pointed his finger at him, laughing reservedly.

"This guy here—he won't be hanging himself either!"

Jerin was inebriated and his anger boiled over immediately.

"What? Explain what you mean?"

The presumptuous teacher, whose bulging eyes looked to be dreaming, suddenly stirred and attempted to get to his feet. He had long since been drunk.

"What do you mean?"

Kačur shook his head and hands in protest.

"No…I won't go around quarrelling!...Not for...I've seen...I'll say nothing more."

"Ass-kisser!" called out the teacher, his voice husky and garbled. And with that he tipped over in his chair.

Jerin looked thoughtful for a while before taking a bottle of water and dabbing his forehead. He said nothing more.

Kačur leaned over the slumbering excise clerk to Matilda and softly placed his hand on hers.

"Miss Matilda...once upon a time...in those early days…"

"Old man, you are drunk!" Matilda interrupted him and pulled her hand away.

Kačur turned away with a dark, offended look on his face. His intoxication stemmed half from the wine and half from repressed and concealed pain that had been born long before this evening in a place far from these faces. He clamped his hands to his head.

"She doesn't like me anymore!"

And he forgot immediately who it was who no longer liked him. The skinny teacher came to mind, and then Matilda, and then his wife, until suddenly his thoughts focused on Minka's creamy face and dark eyes.

He raised his head and gazed around the table at his companions. He stood up slowly, wobbling, his eyes bleary and bulging, and stuck out his arms.

"Who among you all at this table...who among you has loved like this?"

All he could see was unknown faces, intoxicated, staring, and he ceased talking.

Jerin walked over to him and patted him on the shoulder.

"Well...it'll be all right...Now we understand each other."

"Let's sing something!"

"We'll sing some other time. Not tonight."

He brought over Kačur's coat and even set the hat upon his head.

The night air was cool. The sky was strewn with stars, and they were quite close. The road shone as if it were daytime.

Kačur halted. He was rocking and looking up towards the sky.

"How did I lose my way? What land is this?"

He weighed these questions laboriously, and then he hit upon an answer.

"No...They will not entrap me. I have children, and a wife..."

He was talking to himself, and afterwards he began hollering and reeling along the road.

"I have children and a wife!...I've been given enough! There's nothing else I want!...Let me be!...I want to be by myself!"

He stopped again, tested his voice, and then intoned:

> My sweetheart, what have you done?
> Going off to love another...

He fell silent and was suddenly very melancholy.

"Oh, I'm done for! It's almost autumn already, and it'll soon be winter, and what kind of shape is my overcoat in?...What kind of life is this? What's the point?

He arrived at home; a shadow was just alighting from his window.

"Hey, you there!" he exclaimed. He was moving faster now but still staggering. The window rattled forcefully shut.

The shadow stopped in its tracks.

"You just wait! You...know...Stay there...I, I'm not a gentle man!"

He was hunting for his matches and, when he found them, he lit one. He spied in the billowing fog the handsome young man with wheat-colored locks; his smooth skin had gone utterly pallid, and his watery eyes beheld Kačur in dread and horror.

"It's you!" Kačur screamed. The match fell out of his hand and went out.

He motioned with his arm and then sprawled to the ground. The shadow was swallowed up in the night.

The door scraped.

"Is that you, Kačur?"

He picked himself up and reeled in her direction.

"Who was that below the window?"

"Where?"

"Below the window!"

"You drunkard! You've probably been dreaming! Get to bed!"

He shuffled into the foyer.

"Dreaming?" he asked in a sleepy voice. He no longer even knew what he had asked. Dreamily he took off his clothes, smiling beatifically: he was in a garden, and Minka was leaning against the fence.

CHAPTER TWO

By the time Kačur reached his fortieth year, he had become a wizened, stooped old man. He resembled one of those teachers from a long time ago who also worked as a sexton and fluttered around the world like a moth, lost, half-blind, and perpetually irked and mumbling. They have all long been put six feet under, yet here and there a remnant from the past will pop up, part alarming spirit, part pitiful caricature. With short, mincing steps it scoots across the streets in the dark, skinny and bent and bowlegged, its hands aquiver. A threadbare jacket gleams on the elbows and back. The sleeves are too short and the pants too long, and they are tight and wrinkled. A red handkerchief is sticking out of the coat; in the right hand it is holding a thin cane and in the left a snuffbox. Suspicious eyes look out of the beardless, wrinkled visage. Its nose is long and reddened, and tobacco clings to the upper lip. It walks past, sniffing and yammering, looks at the people from the corner of its eye and lashes out at them like a whip with his angry stare. If he sees a tatterdemalion in the street, he lifts his cane at him. Then, suddenly, when he runs into some notable at the corner—mayor, priest or some official—the sagging old body gets some of its pep back. It becomes elastic and youthful, making a bow so deep that its hat scrapes the ground; a smile both merry and officious quivers in the warren of little wrinkles around the mouth and radiates from its eyes.

Now they are all dead and buried...But sometimes, around midnight, a man shows up, gaunt, wearing an old, frayed, unfashionable coat, and he stops in front of the white, single-storied school building. He shakes his head, takes a pinch of tobacco, and then evaporates into the night...

For his favorite retreat Kačur had chosen an out-of-the-way inn that was also a general store. Lumberjacks frequented it, along with farmers up to their ears in debts and professional alcoholics. As long as he was not drunk, Kačur paid no attention to the other guests. He felt comfortable here, and the air was oddly cool, as if he could feel shadows from Blatni Dol on his face. And the people he saw here were all children of the darkness. Crude features, expressionless, inebriated faces, deeply bloodshot eyes, hoarse, raw voices....When the schnapps had gone to his head and loosened his tongue, then his eyes would cruise around the room. They were all there: the mayor from Blatni Dol, and the secretary who spoke German, and the head cottager Samotorec, all the faces he had known for so long. And all the stories they told were familiar from way back, their feuds were old, and never resolved, and everything was just as it had been...Kačur conversed with them, argued with them, explained difficult issues to them, spoke in German and numerous other exotic languages. They listened reverentially to him, because they sensed that he belonged among them. When he was drunk and reeling, he was dragged home by Andrejaz, the young fellow who had no nose, because one time when he was really drunk he had sliced it off himself.

Kačur did not like the sun, or any beam of light. He felt restless and could not focus his eyes, and his head was swimming, and the earth spun under his feat. In his heart arose painful, leaden memories.

One lovely morning he betook himself to the mountains, to the solitary peaks, to get a look at the countryside. It was peaceful up there, but the sun beamed and every blade of grass shone, and the leaves on the bushes and the lonely trees shook softly, enjoying the light. He looked out over the plain. Everything lay in sunlight. Even the fog shimmered; it swept up to the sky in long veils and then melted, sparkling as if it were woven with pearl. The tall houses of Lazi were drenched with gold, so that their windows were in flames. And there was peace, a great and solemn peace, like a holiday…in the distance, a skylark trilled in a field…Kačur stood there, with his head lowered, his eyes blinded by the sun, and his heart rose painfully in his chest as if it were on its way to bursting out of his chest. Vague, half-intelligible thoughts awoke, begotten by the fecund sunlight, stammering thoughts, still timid and unsure of themselves. "I also once…lived that way…in sunshine like that. It wasn't so long ago…When was that? Why couldn't I…? Shouldn't I be able to return to the light?"…He was shaking. He felt like the whole broad, bright landscape was floating up, towards him, and the mountains, the solitary and overheated summits, were rising up to the sky, reaching for the sun itself; and he himself ascended with the fields, mountains, and peaks, and the entire tide of light of the heavens and earth resided in his eyes, in his heart.

Back at home, he lay down on his bed, turned to the wall, and groaned. And never again did he return to the mountaintops of a gorgeous, sunny morning.

He was happiest when he spent time at home alone with his youngest son. He nuzzled him, played right beside him like another child, did handstands on the floor, romped around the apartment and joined him in reconnoitering the secrets of the kitchen and pantry.

It was odd how neither of them laughed very often, and then only briefly, in fits and starts. Their faces stayed serious the whole while, their eyes glazed and unhappy. They played and romped with awkward, childlike movements, swinging their arms wide and resembling two old men who have grown infantile and now pass their time in silly episodes.

Lojze was a weak and sickly child. His belly bulged and his puffy little body rested on legs that were thin, bowed, and uncooperative. His face was covered by skin the color of ashes or water, and large eyes, quiet and shy, looked out from under the high, distended forehead. He was afraid of loud voices, of the hustle and bustle of life, of sunlight; when he was in church, he trembled, pressing his back to the wall as he stared at the people with alarm. He was six years old but could barely walk; his speech was indistinct and he stuttered and wheezed heavily.

If they were playing and the boy's mother came into the room unexpectedly, they immediately fell silent, like two criminals. Lojze would run off and hide.

"Just stick together, you two. At least you enjoy him! He's got it written all over his face that he's the son of a drunk and was born in Blatni Dol!"

He was fond of him, because he was a child of Blatni Dol. To him the boy was like a living shadow, painful and mysterious, something he had been able to rescue when they had been thrust forcibly into the light.

Tone and Francka avoided their father. When Kačur looked into the great, luminous eyes of his son, he gave a noticeable shudder and hung his head, as when he stood before the headmaster. These eyes held something reproachful, dismissive. When they encountered each other on the street, Tone quickly ran away and took refuge around a corner so that he wouldn't have to walk with his father.

"Sit down, Tone! We'll do some schoolwork!" he said once to the boy.

"I do my studying alone!" Tone rejoined stubbornly.

Kačur had wanted to scream at him and had even raised his hand; but then he turned away. His hand fell, and he said nothing at all. Later that year he packed him off to the city to attend the Latin school.

His wife, who earlier had simply been a stranger to him, he now hated with all the quiet, painful power of an impotent heart. He felt humiliated, introverted, and gloomy whenever she was around, but when she turned around and went out through the door or over to the other side of the room, his eyes followed her, filled with deep ill will.

Hatred and rancor were all the stronger in him because he loved her voluptuous body now more than ever. It seemed to him that she showed off her seething, sensual beauty wantonly, gleeful at his pain, as if she sensed that both hatred and love were at work in him.

"How does this blouse look on me?" she asked, standing in front of the mirror and straightening her back so that her breasts pushed up and out. She gave a loud laugh and her eyes sparkled with petulance. Then she twisted coquettishly and glanced over her shoulder at him, so she could catch his dull, hostile look of lust. And then she laughed even more shrilly.

"Hey, Kačur, I think I'm going to the reading room. Are you coming?"

"You mean you'd go alone?"

"Why not? Don't you believe there'll be someone there who can dance with me and walk me home?"

Kačur's mouth twitched.

"I'm coming, too!"

"So come! You'll look great in that tailcoat of yours!"

"Nice. Since we spent everything on your glad rags and on the children. Your children."

"And they aren't yours, too?" she asked with a mischievous grin.

"If they ever were, they aren't any longer."

He fell silent. Then he got to his feet and started speaking in fits and starts as his voice shook.

"Not any more! You even took the children from me!...They don't know who I am or who you are! You—you've taken more out of me than all the others put together!...You robbed me of my soul!...You!..."

She looked at him, dumbfounded.

"Have you gone crazy or what? What have I gotten from you? What did you ever give me?"

He threw on his coat, pulled his hat down onto his head, and ran into the street, pale and trembling.

"Where are you off to, old boy?" The cheery teacher buttonholed him.

"Nowhere!" Kačur looked up at him as if he'd just woken up.

"We already have a new headmaster!"

"Really?"

"His name is Ferjan."

"What?" Kačur gasped.

"Ferjan! He's coming here from Zapolje. He'll arrive tomorrow."

"Ferjan...from Zapolje."

"A solid and thorough man! A pillar of progressive pedagogy!"

"Progressive...? Ferjan?"

"Are you deaf?"

Kačur pulled his hat down farther over his forehead and rushed off to his tavern.

He grabbed a bottle with one shivering hand and emptied it at one go.

"Miracles are occurring on this earth! Divine wonders and portentous signs!...How were things back in the old days? Let's consider this slowly...Well, let's reach back to...Let's go back in time, bit by bit, if we can, and recall how it was."

His head hung low over the table and he rested his forehead on his hands. The schnapps had detonated in his head. Lurid flashing images, too bright, more disturbing than he could handle, unfolded before his eyes.

The rotund shopkeeper chuckled.

"Well, you seem to like the taste of this tonight."

"Bring more."

"So it is Ferjan...that boozer...lickspittle; he said himself he was a lickspittle...'Submit!' he said. 'Give them their due and don't get in their business! And it's better,' he said, 'to be an alcoholic than an idealist.' And now he...what did that dimwit just say? Now he's a 'pillar of the progressive...' Ugh!"

He raised his head, a great smile now plastered across his entire face as if he were a kid, and he turned to the shopkeeper.

"What do you say, Miha? If I had been a drunkard back then, and an idealist now—what would have become of me? Would I be the headmaster today?"

The shopkeeper chuckled amiably, the way he did around drunks who spoke words of wisdom with their sluggish tongues.

"Of course you would!"

Kačur rolled his head to the side and fixed his dull eyes upon the merchant. Through a fog he saw the other man laughing and wobbling to and fro.

"Of course! Maybe inspector by now, too...It's just...A person never knows how to get started on that path, or when...But Ferjan knew...He waited for his hour to come like a cat waits for a mouse. A cat is still...and quiet, doesn't budge, no purring...but then when a mouse appears...Get that bottle over here, Miha!"

He held up his bottle to see whether it was empty. He just as quickly forgot why he had lifted it, and it landed back on the table.

"Some more?" asked the shopkeeper.

Kačur opened his eyes wide, trying to locate him; he caught sight of him behind the counter.

"More!"

He was intoxicated but his thoughts were curiously lucid and spirited and they turned over in his head so fast that he could not follow them; it was as if he were traveling on a fast train through a bright landscape that was tearing past his window.

"Everything in its time…So it is! To be like a rag in the wind…going this way and that and every which way…the wind will deposit you somewhere. Not being a pig-headed little sprout. If it's in loose soil, the wind rips it out and flings it into the furrow. If it's planted deeply, then the wind snaps it off…It's different if no wind is blowing. Then a rag lies there in the mud, while a shoot stretches upwards, into the air. Therefore at that point it is better to be a shoot…People respect you more; they give you more compliments…And so: rag—sprout, sprout—rag… Such his life!"

To a humdrum little melody he began to sing the following words:

"Rag—sprout…Sprout—rag…"

Noseless Andrejaz took him under the arms and walked him home.

The next morning Kačur woke up and thought he remembered a strange dream. Ferjan had been standing there, and he, Kačur, was before him, hat in hand, bowing deeply.

"Was that a dream?" he asked with considerable unease after opening his eyes.

"What do I care about your dreams?" retorted his wife. "You were drunk, and you lay for a while in the foyer."

He put on his Sunday suit and then brushed off his jacket.

"I don't believe it was a dream."

He set out for the school. It was a warm, clear day in autumn. Kačur blinked his clouded eyes. His face was gray and drawn, and his tongue and throat were dry. He found the sunny day disagreeable, because it came across as too sophisticated; it seemed too snobbish for him. He would rather have been walking about in the mud, through rain and darkness.

A *fiaker*[1] had driven up to the school and a gentleman in a light-colored coat hopped out of it and disappeared into the entrance-way.

"It *is* him!" Kačur noted with alarm.

He stopped and then turned around. Something incomprehensible—neither pride nor fear—kept him from showing his face to Ferjan and bowing in greeting just then. He went into the pub and took a seat in a dark corner. He stared at the table. There was a full bottle right before his eyes, but he didn't touch it.

[1] A horse-drawn conveyance used in urban areas, such as Vienna, where they are still known as *Fiaker*. The Slovene word used here is *koloselj*; the *fiaker* is also known in French and English as a *caleche*.

He sat there for a long time. Then he buried his face in his hands and felt the tears burning his eyes.

"This is not just! God's ways cannot lead in this direction!…Suffering without recompense…recompense without suffering!"

The bottle was still full when he left. He returned to school with a more determined stride and a frown on his face.

Ferjan was coming down the steps, engaged in a loud conversation with Jerin.

"Ah, so there you are, Kačur! I was looking for you, but they told me…Well—" and he held out his hand, "so how are you? You've aged quite a bit, it's true. If I had run into you on the street, I wouldn't have recognized you!"

"It is what it is," Kačur said with a bitter smile. "One rises, and one falls…That's what makes the world go 'round…"

"Say what?" Ferjan laughed. "Surely you aren't envious of me? You know what, old chap? Let's go somewhere and talk about the old days. It's still a long time till lunch."

Jerin gave Ferjan his hand.

"You aren't coming along? Well, all right. Goodbye…What is it? Why are you giving me such a nasty look, Kačur?"

"I don't give any other kind. I've kicked the habit," Kačur answered as the self-confidence that had come to life in his heart melted away.

They entered the pub and found a place to sit in the formal dining room.

Ferjan sighed. "Of course, back there in Blatni Dol…Why were you so stupid? Look, I'm a couple of years older than you, and you, on the other hand, are much brighter than I.—What has happened to you, and what has happened with me?"

"Just tell me," Kačur said, looking him intently in the eyes, "how you do it. I would like to know…because I don't understand it. I just cannot fathom it. I set my sights so low, did such innocent things back then, and yet now: ruin. But they call you a pillar of progressive pedagogy and now…headmaster. See, I don't get this! Explain it to me!"

Kačur was speaking sincerely, guilelessly, to him, with probing eyes and obvious strain on his face.

Ferjan guffawed.

"Back there in Zapolje, you were a child, and you were a child in Blatni Dol, and, believe it or not, you are still a child!…Don't you get it? Back then, twelve years ago, one wasn't allowed to be progressive…and now it's permitted! It's even profitable to be so!"

"So what is one not permitted to be nowadays?"

"You always want to be what is off limits?"

"No!" Kačur shook his head swiftly and held up his hands. "I don't aspire to be anything—neither what's allowed nor what isn't."

"Nothing at all, then?"

"Nothing!"

"Not a teacher, either? People are giving me dismal reports about your methods. You must have brought them with you from Blatni Dol…But never mind; we are in a pub here!"

Kačur grew fearful. He no longer saw Ferjan opposite him, but rather a boss, and one with a grave look on his face and severity in his voice.

"Sir, I…" he sputtered.

"What?" Ferjan was studying him, bewildered.

"That's not what I meant…I did not mean to offend you…" Kačur excused himself in a timorous voice.

"What the hell is wrong with you? Have you snapped?" marveled Ferjan. "I just wanted to put that school issue on the table…That can be cleared up. But you're cranky and depressed. Cancer is eating at your heart—hence the cane and curses in the classroom. It's obvious—how about trying to be pleasant?"

"But I will endeavor…Look, Ferjan, now I can see that you're a good man…I will make an effort!"

"Basta! Who could listen to more of this? I understand how someone in your shoes could change, but to turn into an old hag—no way!" Ferjan's blood was boiling now.

Kačur no longer knew what to say or how he should justify himself.

"Forgive me, Ferjan…This life is very difficult for me!—The things I have experienced, all that I've seen since I left Blatni Dol—it's all so unfamiliar, irregular. I don't know what is to be done."

He stared at the table.

"It wasn't right for them to drive me out of Blatni Dol…I had already made a home there…I was putting in the transfer requests out of habit—and because I was happy each time they were turned down…It wasn't right of me to keep asking for one…There I could've died in peace!"

Ferjan gave him a sympathetic look, but his sympathy was laced with a healthy dose of derision.

"You've been weak."

"No, it wasn't weakness, Ferjan. It's only now, when I think back about it, it's only now that I realize how much strength used to be in me. But, drop by drop…ad infinitum…you reach the bottom of any barrel, no matter how big…But you don't know anything! About what things are like out there! A man tries just to shake it off and get back to business! But those things…the suffering behind closed doors—that no friend, or anyone else in the world, can see, for which no compensation is ever paid. You should experience that, Ferjan!"

"Well…of course."

It was obvious that Ferjan was bored.

"And on other fronts? How is your wife?"

"How should she be?" Kačur parried the question. "She feels at home here already. But I don't."

Both men fell silent.

"It will be lunchtime soon, I think," said Ferjan, checking his watch.

"Yes, it's time." And Kačur stood up.

"Are you coming to the reading room tomorrow?"

"Perhaps."

"Your wife as well?"

Kačur looked at him and muttered: "Of course, she'll be there."

When he got home that day, his thoughts were more agitated and his heart more choked up than usual.

"It's not just me, dear brother. You've changed too. And even if you're wearing a new suit these days, your changes have been as baleful as mine!"

His wife was mending and ironing her things. She laid out her blouse, as well as her skirt and hat. Her face looked feverish and she barely glanced at Kačur.

"Are you really going?" she asked casually, toting the hot iron in from the kitchen.

"Yes. Wherever you go, I'm going," Kačur answered with a sardonic smile. He studied the flattened skirt being pressed under her moving iron; he scrutinized the blouse hanging on the door and the lacy white undergarments.

"Who are you getting so decked out for?"

"Most likely not for you!"

He beheld her full, exposed throat and her powerful, bare arms and quivered. He seized her shoulder and sensed the heat from her body.

"Why do you treat me this way?"

"Leave me alone. Can't you see that I'm working?"

He stood for another moment behind her. He had lifted his hand from her shoulder and now held it, clenched spasmodically like a claw, above her neck.

"If only I could choke...just squeeze..."

Her head shifted and she was banging around with the iron. His hand dropped away. He slouched off to his room, deeply hunched over, shaking, and he lay down on the bed fully dressed.

"Even those things I've received as paltry compensation—even they don't belong to me. Weak, he said I am weak...and very much so. Why didn't I strike? Choke?"

From the bed along the wall, two wide open, runny eyes were fixed on him.

"Papa!"

He sprang over to the wall and took the boy into his arms.

"You...You belong to me! Tell me, whose are you?"

"Papa's!"

"Of course you're mine...And you are so sick, you poor thing!"

She stood there in the middle of the room, a vision in lace and silk ribbons, with a long feather in her hat and a white parasol in her hand. He took her measure with his eyes and she no longer seemed so beautiful to him. Only her blushing, merry face still seemed pretty.

"Are you coming, too?" she asked.

"I'll be along later."

"What is that look on your face? Don't you think I'm pretty?"

"No!"

"What a tremendous shame that I don't suit you." With that she turned around. "Lock the door behind me!"

He continued to watch as she rustled past the window and opened the parasol to keep the evening sun from shining on her face. As he watched her like that, he noticed for the first time that her gloves were too tight and a touch too short underneath the ends of her sleeves as well.

He himself did not set out until it was dark.

His path led past the tavern, his shadowy and pleasant home away from home.

"Wouldn't I rather just pop in there? Who will rebuke me for anything here? Who will bark orders at me in there? Is anybody here going to shred this tired, tired soul?"

And into the bar he walked, before he had time to answer his own questions.

"Looking spiffy tonight!" said the grocer. "Off to the reading room, perhaps?"

"Off to the reading room," Kačur grumbled in reply.

"Solo? No wife?"

"She's already there."

"Aha. So she already left."

The chubby merchant's face brightened and then broke out in a derisive smile.

"She went, just like that?"

Kačur gave him a morose look.

"What's with the laugh? And why do you ask?"

"Well...!" the grocer shrugged his shoulders. "Asking is free!"

At another table sat a farmer, quite in his cups, who was a regular customer there. He was smoking a short pipe, staring boldly at Kačur, and smiling coyly to himself. At last he plucked the pipe from his mouth, spat, and smiled for all he was worth: "You're well-educated enough, schoolmaster, to speak both German and Italian...but you don't get what's going on right before your eyes!"

"What's that supposed to mean?" Kačur responded irately.

"It's not supposed to mean anything! When I have an itch, I scratch it. And I know how to delouse my own hair."

Kačur quickly drained his glass and left.

The play was already over, and the singing was almost finished, when Kačur walked through the door and glanced into the hall. In the second row from the stage, seated on the red velvet, was his wife: happy, proud, blushing. Neither her twinkling eyes nor her ardent countenance, bubbling over with life, contained a whiff of the existence of Blatni Dol. The lace around her neck and wrists, and the laughter that was just a touch too loud, scarcely betrayed a hint of it either. Next to her sat that young clerk, the fop with the wheat-colored hair, soft skin, and unflattering turn of mouth.

"She has not noticed me," thought Kačur. And if she glances this way, she still wouldn't see me...But just you wait!"

Ice rose up in his breast; gall flooded his entire body and spilled out onto his face.

"Just wait!...You'll see the real me yet!...You are going to be down on your knees, wringing your hands and staring up at me, wide-eyed! Just wait, you bitch!"

The song they had been singing upon stage was over. Still blushing and clapping, a happy Tončka was laughing beatifically, like a child, and looking about. Her hands stopped and fell in mid-air. The blood drained from her cheeks and lips. She had caught sight of his face, and never before had she seen it like this: a blood-curdling face, surrounded by darkness, pale and twisted.

Kačur spun around.

In the bar attached to the hall, he got a rowdy reception. Ferjan got to his feet behind his table.

"We thought you weren't going to make it, Kačur! It took a lot of doing, but I convinced them that you're not a conservative, or a sycophant, or an informer. Have a seat! Here, sit right next to me...What's wrong?"

Kačur was still pale and quaking.

"I had an attack of nausea, that's all. What's the occasion for tonight's celebration?"

"Occasion?" Ferjan chuckled. "Why does everything have to have a purpose? It's just a party. They hold one every year, and so they're holding it this year, too. You still can't let go of those days when every word had to be meaningful."

Inside a cloud of tobacco smoke, down at the end of the table, the mayor sat, looking gaily at Kačur from under his beetling brows.

"You've gone through some tough times, and they've still got their claws in you!"

Kačur was annoyed by the large, fashionable soiree. He felt himself to be small and clumsy. So he drank rapidly, and the wine went to his head.

"Tonight you will not escape us!" Ferjan said cheerfully. "Tonight you have to tell us what it's been like! Be happy, and open up a little bit! Take a look at us—aren't we all decent folks?"

"Leave me alone, Ferjan! Why are you making fun of me? I am too old for this!"

Ferjan leaned far back in his chair, exhaled a dense cloud of smoke and looked quizzically at Kačur.

"I don't think it's just that you've aged, Kačur."

"What else then?"

Ferjan kept his eyes on him and smiled disdainfully.

"Back then, when nothing came at a cost to you, when you were young and single, it was easy to march to your own drummer."

Kačur located his glass with a trembling hand and drained it. Jerin placed his hand on Ferjan's shoulder.

"No, Ferjan....It's not like that."

Ferjan shrugged him off; it was the alcohol in him talking.

"In those days—ha! Young, single, who cares about the future! Now: Mr. Priest, sir!—Your hat scrapes the ground. Mr. Mayor, sir!—You bow till your head bangs your belt! Mr. Headmaster, sir!—Hey, Jerin, did you know that my friend here, Kačur, addressed me as "Director" and "Sir"? Although we are friends[2] and have been co-workers?"

Kačur was shaking. His face had completely blanched and his cheekbones protruded.

"Ferjan! Why?" he asked with trembling voice and bloodshot eyes.

"We're onto you! You're a Clerical!"

"I'm a what?" Kačur said, astonished. He looked around the table.

"A Clerical!" Ferjan said with a laugh.

The singing in the theater was at an end, and the crowd now poured into the lounge. Kačur glimpsed his

[2] The verb Cankar uses to express a condition of friendship here, here, *tikati*, expresses an informal or intimate relationship between two speakers who know each other well and use the word *ti* for each other instead of the more formal *vi*. This concept is familiar to speakers of continental European languages; a vestige of it in English is the older pronoun "thou."

wife at the side of the curly-headed young man; he saw the slender schoolteacher with the tall, goateed clerk, and he heard the forwarding agent's wife and her prattling voice. But he perceived it all as if it were rocking in the fog, as if in a dream.

Music started up back in the main hall and couples began standing up. His wife had stood up, too; he saw her behind his back though he had not turned around to face her.

"Why aren't you going over to dance?" Ferjan grinned at him.

Kačur just gawked.

"Your wife is dancing now!"

Kačur took a swig and said nothing.

"You pantywaist! Oh, such a weakling!" Ferjan snarled with disgust and spat on the floor.

"Who's a weakling?" Kačur asked in a low, hoarse voice.

"You. You are!" Ferjan yelled. He ridiculed Kačur with his laugh.

Kačur did turn around, slowly, but his hand was shaking so much that he spilled his glass of wine. He turned back to face Ferjan. Breathing heavily, he said in a subdued voice: "It's you, Ferjan. You are an ass-kisser! You are the pantywaist!"

"Do you know who you're talking to?" Ferjan blustered.

"To a sycophant! To a toady! I remember your exact words: if you turned us inside out, you and me—what would you have? I'd be a meter taller than you. A meter, ha—try a hundred meters! Nowadays you are the pillar, o pitiful pillar! And who provided the pedestal that lets you stand and rise? Who—if not me, through my suffering? You were a weakling and a yes-man and a drunkard back when I was chiseling this pedestal with my bloody sweat. This pedestal you now occupy like such a he-man!—What was it you said? 'Nowadays a person can become anything at all!'"

Jerin fixed his bright eyes on Kačur and rejoined: "Socialist!"

"Indeed! God only knows what that is, but to spite you, Ferjan, I'm a Socialist! What you are today, I was fifteen years ago. Why? Because I wasn't permitted to be that then, because it required sacrifice. What I fertilized with my blood, you have reaped…You thief!"

Ferjan had turned pale. He gnawed his lips.

The last notes of the waltz in the concert hall faded.

"Do you see your wife?" Ferjan asked with a wild rictus of scorn.

"What does my wife matter to you?" Kačur answered through clinched teeth. He did not turn around.

"I have danced with her, too."

Kačur stared at Ferjan and his eyes began glazing over.

"I kissed her, too. On your wedding night!"

Kačur shot to his feet, swaying. He grabbed his glass and hurled it at Ferjan's face.

Arms enveloped him, someone threw his coat over his shoulders, and someone else put his hat on his head and, the next thing he knew, he was on the street.

Jerin placed a firm hand on his arm.

"I'll see you home. You were right…Ferjan was drunk!"

Kačur tore himself free.

"Get away! I can't stand any of you. Stay away from me!"

Jerin remained in the entrance-way, watching as Kačur hurried along the street and disappeared in the dark…

Slowly, absorbed in thought, Jerin went back up the steps. He looked into the concert hall as he walked past. Tončka was dancing with Ferjan, who was talking very loudly, laughing, and starting to stagger.

CHAPTER THREE

Ferjan and Kačur were sitting in the conference room. Kačur cowered there with his hands upon his knees. His face looked old and clay-colored, and his blood-rimmed eyes were dull.

Ferjan, already rather corpulent, starting to gray, was visibly nervous and uncomfortable. He crumpled a piece of paper in his hand and stared at the table.

"We were once colleagues," he said, taking a quick peek at Kačur's profile next to him. "Colleagues and friends! By God, I did not violate this friendship, and whenever some stupidity got in the way, we took care of it as appropriate. But, look here, Mr. Kačur—"

Their eyes met, and neither man lowered his gaze.

"—This can break up a friendship, too!...Until a couple of years ago, I looked at you with the same regard I had earlier, so very long ago, when you towered above us all...When we still hoped that someday you would...Well, that's over now...We'll speak no more of it...I am not asking you which political camp you belong to. That's your affair and your problem. I'm nothing but your headmaster now..."

"What's he getting at?" Kačur thought to himself. "Ah, I know what he's going to say!"

"I have told you this in order that you will expect no further…special considerations from me. The final favor I can do for you, instead of reporting you, which is actually what is required here…is to give you some advice…Do you know what I mean?"

"I know," Kačur said with his worn-out smile.

Ferjan stood up and moved closer to Kačur. His mien was earnest but still friendly, full of sympathy.

"For God's sake, Kačur, is there no hope for you? Find fault with us, make fun of the reading room, of the choral society, and ultimately you can be a socialist, or an anarchist, whatever you want…but behave like a good Christian soul! Why do we have to have these scandals in the school? You know word of it will leak out…and people will be writing about it soon! Some farmer will come along with a cudgel because you thrashed his son. You, who were once the Evangelist—no offence intended!…But of course if you are always drunk…Drink at night, I implore you, when no one can see you, but be sober again by morning! Must you drink during the day? All day?…You should be ashamed…"

Ferjan bit his lip anxiously and took a step backwards.

"You know yourself[1] what I'm trying to say. So conform, I beg you!" His voice had grown colder, but he did stick out his hand in Kačur's direction.

"You're right. You're right!" Kačur nodded, shook the other man's hand, and walked out.

[1] Ferjan has now switched to the formal mode of address in his verbs and pronouns, employing the Slovene verb *vikati*. Cf. Note 2 in Part 3, Chapter 2.

"One thing is especially worth recalling here," Kačur thought. "Earlier, people used to ask me all sorts of questions about what I did at home, what I ate, drank, whom I talked with, what political views I held, whether I went to church and confession, all about the way I lived in general.—And lo and behold! Now someone comes along and inquires about what I do in the school! Just imagine—in school! At one time it seemed to me that that was worthy of respect...I thought it was a noble and holy profession...Now, when was that exactly? Bah, may the past rest in peace! But now, suddenly, like a spirit escaping in the night from a grave: what is going on at school? Wouldn't you know it, those urchins have souls...! Really, such a momentous question, and very noble, and therefore it must be taken under consideration."

He walked into the pub, sat down in the darkest corner, and flipped up the collars of his greatcoat.

"Just get that brandy over here! Ferjan says I shouldn't drink. It's just the thing, then!"

His thoughts were sluggish and exhausting. They dragged themselves past, like mists over the plain, vague and formless.

"Just look at how he put on airs in front of me! Who is he?...What can he do to me? How can he lay a hand on me? Just let him try something!"

He drank, wrapping himself up ever tighter in the coat, in his collar. A cold winter wind whipped up the loose snow and chased it into the tavern whenever the door opened. Today was the final school day before Christmas. Ever since morning, a dusk-like grayness had lain over the village, and early in the afternoon it grew altogether dark. Snow, fine and cold, was dropping from the lowering heavens. It came down more and more heavily and rose up to the level of windows, and even roofs when there were gusts.

Soon Kačur had forgotten Ferjan, but he felt with renewed and redoubled impact the silent dread in his heart that had gripped him of late with its hands of iron. He finished his drink, buttoned up his coat, and hurried home.

"For whom are you making this tea?" he asked his wife.

She did not look at him.

"Why are you here so early tonight?"

Kačur spit onto the floor and walked into the next room. Lojze lay down on the low, crude bed in the darkness. His breath rattled and came slowly. Kačur lit the lamp. The child sought his father with his large, clear, and singularly bright eyes, and he held out his thin little arms.

"What did you bring me, Papa?"

Kačur pulled some carob-beans, figs, and pieces of candy from his coat.

"Here you go, Lojze! Hold out your hands!"

Lojze laboriously lifted his head, cupped his hands, and let out a laugh just like he used to. But it was quiet and quick, and then his sickly, prematurely old face grew earnest again. He was ten years old, but his body was small and weak like that of a five-year old, and it was lost under the blanket. His bulging forehead loomed ever more over the rest of his small, hollow face and his sunken, sparkling eyes.

The boy placed the offerings on the blanket, without tasting the carob-beans, figs, or candy.

"Daddy!"

Kačur bent close to him.

"Daddy! Come right up to my mouth…so that Mama doesn't hear!"

Kačur bent all the way down to the boy's lips. He felt Lojze's hot breath on his face.

"Daddy," whispered the boy, his breathing loud and constricted. "Tell me if it's true. Am I really going to die?"

A chill swept through Kačur's entire body, and even his heart recoiled.

He wrapped Lojze in the blanket, took him in his arms, and pressed him to his chest.

"Who's been saying things like that to you, Lojze?"

"Mama said it," the boy whispered. He flung both arms around his father's neck. "Am I really going to die, Papa?"

"You will not die! I won't allow it!"

He was not only comforting the boy but also defending himself from the cold horror that constricted his own heart whenever he saw the small, bowed, broken down body of his son, or glimpsed his gray, ageing face, or whenever his eyes met the timid, moribund, troubled gaze of the boy.

He paced back and forth, rocking the boy in his arms.

"Why are you thinking about bad words like that, Lojze? Don't listen to them, and if you hear them, forget them! How could you die, Lojze, when I love you? It will soon be Christmas, and I'm going to build you a creche. I'll build it myself—a beautiful manger scene!"

"Just for me?"

"Just for you, Lojze! I'll put it right there, in the corner next to the bed. And you can take the raisins from the cake and put them in it, so that the shepherds have something to bring to the Christ child in the night!"

"Last year I did that, too, but Tone ate them up while I was sleeping."

"He won't eat them this year! I'm going to sit by your bed and keep watch all night long, so that nothing happens. And if you should wake up and can't get back to sleep, we'll talk for a little while…"

"Will you tell me about the city, Papa? I want so badly to go to the city, like Tone…"

His eyes gleamed with a supernatural light, as if they spotted in the distance an unknown miracle, some remote thing of beauty that not everyone was entitled to see.

"You'll get to go to the city, too, Lojze, and you'll be a great gentleman…and you'll still be fond of me, even if you are modern and sophisticated, and you won't avoid me, or give me nasty looks like Tone does!"

"I'll always like you, Papa!"

He placed the boy in bed, tucked his arms under the blanket, and covered him up to his neck.

"Go to sleep now, Lojze! Don't think about those bad things. And don't let them into your dreams. Tomorrow morning when you wake up, you'll be well, and we'll play together like we used to do!"

Lojze fixed him with his frightened eyes.

"Are you going away, Papa? Don't leave…not tonight!"

The voice amidst those sobs betrayed an extraordinary anxiety. He pulled his hands from under the blanket and stretched them out towards his father.

"I'm not going anywhere, Lojze! I'll always be close by and I'll be listening out for you the entire time!...But for now go to sleep! Be a good boy and stick your arms back under the blanket so you don't freeze. Close those eyes, think about Christmas, and about Easter, and you'll drift right off to sleep!"

Lojze partially closed his eyes. He watched his father from under thick lashes.

Kačur went into the other room, quietly closing the door behind him.

"Who came by to visit?" he asked in a whisper.

"Who do you think was here? Nobody has been here!" His wife's voice was surly and sharp.

"Not so loud! The boy has to sleep!—I heard the outside door open and somebody walk into the room. You talked with him and he left...Who was it? Those were a man's footsteps."

The spite and disgust in her sneer defied measure. She looked him straight in the eye and imitated his whisper:

"Really? A man's footsteps? Stop the presses! How did you guess that? It's a wonder you still know what a man's footsteps sound like!"

"Who was it?"

"What, is nobody allowed to enter our house anymore? Leave me alone!"

Deep hatred was visible in her eyes. It was matched by the hatred in his. They paled: one beast staring down the other...But it only lasted an instant and then both of them wavered.

Kačur returned to his son in the other room. The lamp was turned down and its light danced drowsily. He went over to the bed and bent down. Lojze was breathing quietly, but heavily and at considerable intervals. Beneath his half-shut lids, the whites of his eyes stared forth. Perspiration cloaked his forehead; a cold sweat lay on his hands.

"He's gone to sleep!"

Kačur tiptoed across the room, turned the lamp down even further, took a chair to the edge of the bed, and sat down.

"But this just can't be! God cannot be so unmerciful as to take this away from me, too!"

In the half-light he beheld the little face below him, gray, old before its time, and it seemed to him that on it was inscribed the story of his life—its mute, despicable suffering.

In the uncanny silence, the twilight, and clammy air, memories arose in his heart more plainly, more distinctly than ever before, in his agitated heart that was waking up to the real meaning of dread. He looked at himself in the mirror and recoiled in fright.

Once a young man had set out into the world, light of foot and with his heart filled with hope. And not just hope, but an infinite, all-encompassing love. He went and offered the people something of his riches, of his love. "Just look at that outlaw—he's offering us love.—Stone him!" And they thronged around him and hurled rocks and filth[2] at him until he collapsed. And when he arose, he moved on, across the mountains, and there he offered to the people of his wealth, of his love. "Just look at that bandit! He's offering us love.—Stone him!" And they encircled him and hurled rocks and filth at him, until he collapsed...But then a miracle occurred: one handful of filth landed in his heart, and it surged and waxed until it filled his entire breast, right to the top; it was heavy and so the wanderer's steps were no longer bouncy and light as before; his back was bowed and his head sank down. And at that point a second miracle took place: from the moment the filth had landed in his heart, he ceased to yearn for the heights, or for distant horizons. He now loved the swamp, the darkness of the damp forests, the murky ravines, muffled and forgotten and hidden away in the mountains. And then a third wonder transpired: the people who had once stoned him were now standing at the edge of the forest, in the warmest sun imaginable, by the marshlands where the earth was firmest, on the rims of the gorges, and higher up on the mountain path, and they were pointing their fingers at him.

"Look! There's the one who has no love in his heart!" And when he heard their laughter, he was on the brink of tears, and—.

Kačur's bitterness was so great that he shuddered.

A timid thought arose in him, hesitant and quivering, like a firefly in the blackness.

[2] The word Kačur uses here is *blato*, "filth" or "mud," as in the name of the village Blatni Dol.

"Is it no longer possible to…?"

"Papa!" came a whisper from the bed.

Kačur started. He saw the two great, stricken eyes, totally white. He rushed over to the table, adjusted the lamp, and returned to the boy's bedside.

"What can I do for you, Lojze?" He bent over his son, right down to his lips.

Those lips were moving, and the wide-open eyes were fixed on him.

A cold shiver hit Kačur. He took the child by the shoulders and raised his head.

"What do you need, Lojze? Just say something!"

His head fell back. The thin, bony arms lay on top of the blanket.

"This can't be true!" Kačur screamed in horror. "You can't die, Lojze!"

He lifted the boy out of the bed and held him tight. His cheeks were still warm, and his unruffled brow still bore a layer of sweat.

"Look at me, Lojze," Kačur entreated, his legs trembling. "Just look at me, even if you can't say anything!"

His thin arms hung lifelessly at his side; his lips were still.

Kačur unlatched the door and then used his foot to push it open wide.

"Wife! See here!" he cried, his voice hoarse and strangely changed.

She came closer; her face remained distant, tranquil.

"Why are you screaming? He's dead! Put him on the bed."

"Dead?" Kačur shrieked. Staring straight ahead, transfixed, he was still pressing the little body to his own.

After the bed was arranged properly, Kačur remained sitting there all night, next to his immobile, pale son. All night and all of the following day.

A piece of his heart had been torn away, and part of his life had drowned in the night. But this portion of his life had been the dearest to him; it was the entire legacy of his past, the whole share of happiness that tight-fisted fate had vouchsafed him: the memories of sin and humiliation…When he regarded that small pale face, quiet on its bed, and the thin, claw-like hands, folded, he sensed with terror how much he had lost to this death, and it was with terror that he sensed the reasons why he had clung with such great love to that sick little body living in the dark…It was a living shadow, slowly ebbing away, voiceless, yielding to its affliction, a shadow from Blatni Dol…A reminder of sin and humiliation.

He was sitting by the bed, scowling and grim, when someone opened the door to his temple.

"Where to? What now?" he pondered in deep-seated anxiety, like a child who has lost his mother and finds himself on an unfamiliar street among unknown people.

"There's no path leading anywhere, and why should I keep going, anyhow? Where?"

Tone had entered the room; he'd come home for the Christmas holiday. He was dressed stylishly, in the manner of the city: a light-colored tie around his neck, with his hair neatly combed, his face soft and smooth, his lips firmly set and self-assured. He looked at the dead boy with calm curiosity.

"Just look—he's dead." Kačur said, his voice cracking, as if he were revealing to his son a devastating piece of news.

"Yeah, I can see that. What kind of life would he have had, anyway, if he had lived?"

He turned around and went out to where his mother was, while Kačur covered the boy's face…

It was dark in the room. The candle guttered, its light popping and waving; the eternal restlessness of the shadows propelled them swiftly over the ceiling, around the walls, across the face of the deceased. Outside it was snowing; the wind howled so hard that the windows were rattling. In the other room the clinking of glasses and cups was audible, along with conversation in low but animated tones and occasional bursts of laughter that flew out and banged against the door like the snow at the windows.

"They refuse to let him sleep!" Kačur grew livid and opened the door.

At the table sat his wife and Tone with that foppish clerk, who had a moronic look on his face and thick, sneering lips. The pot of tea on the table was steaming; the cups were full.

Kačur turned on the civil servant. "What are you doing here, at a time like this?"

"What does it matter?" his wife answered. "I invited him to tea."

The official gave a slight, sardonic grin and stood up.

"You just stay!" the woman howled.

"Be gone! Get out of here at once!"

The man took one look at Kačur's face, straightened up, and threw on his coat. Kačur held the door for him and then slammed it shut as he left.

"And who is that man?" he inquired of his wife in a shaky voice. She was also trembling but stared straight back into his eyes.

"You should have asked him!"

"Have you no heart, that you would invite him here tonight, of all nights?"

"Don't you worry about my heart! You've never concerned yourself with it before, and you don't need to start now."

He looked at her standing there before him, all sensuality and stubbornness, and the rage wrung from him by long years of suffering rose up and stuck in his throat:

"Whore!"

A dark red pall came over her face.

"Say it again."

"Whore!"

She stared at him in silence. Suddenly her face became calm, even as her lips curled into a glare of contempt and disgust.

"Who would not have turned into a whore, living with you? Did you ever make me happy?...And even if I'd taken up with a hundred men, or more, you couldn't criticize me for it. The world can pass judgment on me, and God will do so, too—but you don't have the right! You are the only one who has no right!"

Kačur's breath came laboriously now and he could barely bring himself to speak.

"A whore—and you confess this publicly?"

"For all to hear!" his wife screeched. "To everyone, if it has to be that way! Call the whole village together, get them all to come over here, and I'll point to every man who's paid me a visit. I am beyond desire.—And I am beyond fear. I won't hide it from you any longer. All the blame falls on your shoulders. What have you given me from day one, right up till tonight? Suffering, suffering, endless suffering...If I wasn't good enough for you, then why did you take me? Just because I was a serving girl, did that mean that God had given you the right to kill me—slowly—to kill me off, piece by piece? To lock me up in this prison, where I cried for ten years till God Himself rescued me?—Whore? You got that right. What else have I ever been to you? Was I ever a wife in your eyes? Someone with whom you felt happy? Did you ever introduce me to other people and say, 'Here, this is my wife?'—Oh, you liked me at night, but then when daylight came you no longer acknowledged me...Whore! That's right! I did what you wanted of me!"

She was panting hard; her eyes welled with tears and red splotches appeared on her face.

Their son sat at the opposite side of the table from them. He was completely pale and his whole body trembled as he listened.

Kačur was petrified. The room swam before his eyes.

"You lie!" he blurted out, lurching towards her with his fist raised. Their son leapt over to them and grabbed Kačur's arm.

"Leave Mother alone!"

Kačur looked at the pale young face confronting him. Deranged with horror for a moment, he thought that he recognized it: it was his own face. The face of the man he had once been—the countenance of the man who had once sallied forth into the world with a heart full of hope.

"Let go of me."

The son released his father's arm and it dropped down. Kačur drew so close to his son's face that they were almost touching.—When Tone saw the strange flicker in his father's eyes, he drew back in alarm.

"Listen!" Kačur said haltingly, his voice almost a whisper. "I'm going to tell you something. Only you. Someday, if things start going badly for you, as they have for me, and filial piety leads you to think back on me, you will not need to feel soiled by my memory. You will cry a blood-laced tear for every kind word that you never shared with me. I forgive you—for you will also go this route and God only knows whether filth will also get poured into your heart. It's written all over your face: you'll start out on this path, and then from time to time you'll be reminded of me...Do you understand what I'm telling you?"

He forced his lips into a strange, child-like smile. His son just stared at him as fear rose up in his gut.

Kačur went into the next room, where he kissed his deceased son on both cheeks, drained the wax from the candle so that it would burn more brightly, and put on his overcoat.

"Where are you going, Papa?" his son asked.

Kačur walked across the room, smiling but saying nothing.

"Don't stop him! Let him go wherever he wants!"

He opened the door.

"That's what it's come to. There's the last word: 'Let him go wherever he wants!'"

And without a word of farewell, he left.

The wind was blowing outside, and snow was falling, but he felt strangely warmed.

"This is how it was twenty years ago," he thought with a smile. "Alone…Free!…But now I have acquired bitter experience; now I will know which path is the right one."

He laughed heartily.

"Oh, now I'll now longer sing the Credo when we're at the Gloria. The first thing is to cultivate an understanding of people, of their times, the conditions, and then, cautiously, on your tiptoes…One must act in accordance with the times, not with one's own ideas. And when there's no wind, you have to wait till it picks up…But if a person is headstrong…and pushes ahead on his own…he'll accomplish nothing. You'll just slip down in the mud. If he orients himself to others, he can twiddle his thumbs while time works in his favor…So it is! I was attempting to sow in the autumn and reap in the spring. Well, well, well!" He stopped in the street as the snow flew past him. "I should have told my son all of this…How will he get along, the poor boy, without the benefit of such lessons?"

His legs carried him into the tavern, but it was only when the brandy stood before him that he noticed he was in his regular haunt.

"Why so bouncy, schoolmaster?" the merchant marveled. "Didn't your son pass away?"

"He did die! He died!" Kačur smiled and rubbed his hands. "They've all died. Including my wife!"

The guests all turned to look at him.

"All of them!" He laughed and took a drink. "Now I am on my own. All alone. Now you will see what I'm made of."

He finished off his schnapps, pulled his coat tighter around him, and headed back out into the street.

Outside the village, on the main road, the wind was fiercer. It whirled clouds of snow high up into the dark sky.

The wind lashed Kačur's face, carried off his hat, and even blew open his coat.

"Ha!" he thought, grinning as he staggered along with great effort. "The weather was nicer the first time I started out...The sun was shining..."

The wind had unbuttoned his coat, sailed inside it, and driven him to the side of the road. Kačur lost control, waving his hands about in the air...and then his blood spattered onto a mile-marker and began oozing down into the snow...

"I wanted to do good. Forgive me!" He smiled and stretched out his hand. He reached out because the blacksmith, the one who had once been left lying on the road with a shattered skull, was bending down towards him. He had grabbed Kačur under the arms and stood him upright. The smith's face was pale, and compassionate, and blood was trickling across his forehead and into his eyes...